"I'm wondering why I like you so much, even though you're obviously lying to me."

Flynn pulled Tess in a little bit closer. "I'm not lying to you," she said softly. *Not about this.* "I just should have forgotten the whole thing and…and…what are you doing?"

Somehow he had moved in closer and all but buried his nose against her neck. "You smell good," he said. "Like cinnamon and sugar and soap."

Flynn didn't smell so bad himself. His scent was masculine and it teased her senses in a way she hadn't expected. But she wasn't about to tell him so.

"I don't have time for this," she whispered.

"Neither do I," he said, "and still I'm sitting here thinking…why not?"

Dear Reader,

June brings you six high-octane reads from Silhouette Intimate Moments, just in time for summer. First up, Ingrid Weaver enthralls readers with *Loving the Lone Wolf* (#1369), which is part of her revenge-ridden PAYBACK miniseries, Here, a street thug turned multimillionaire on a mission falls for the enemy's girlfriend and learns that looks can be deceiving! Crank up your air-conditioning as Debra Cowan's miniseries THE HOT ZONE will definitely raise temperatures with its firefighter characters. The second book, *Melting Point* (#1370), has a detective heroine and firefighting hero discovering more than one way to put out a fire as they track a serial killer.

Caridad Piñeiro lures us back to her haunting miniseries, THE CALLING. In *Danger Calls* (#1371), a beautiful doctor loses herself in her work, until a heady passion creates delicious chaos while throwing her onto a dangerous path. You'll want to curl up with Linda Winstead Jones's latest book, *One Major Distraction* (#1372), from her miniseries LAST CHANCE HEROES, in which a marine poses as a teacher to find a killer and falls for none other than the fetching school cook…who hides one whopper of a secret.

When a SWAT hero butts heads with a plucky reporter, a passionate interlude is sure to follow in Diana Duncan's *Truth or Consequences* (#1373), the next book in her fast-paced miniseries FOREVER IN A DAY. In *Deadly Reunion* (#1374), by Lauren Nichols, our heroine thinks her life is comfortable. But of course, mayhem ensues as her ex-husband—a man she's never stopped loving—returns to solve a murder and clear his name…and she's going to help him.

This month is all about finding love against the odds and those adventures lurking around the corner. So as you lounge in your favorite chair, lose yourself in one of these gems from Silhouette Intimate Moments!

Sincerely,

Patience Smith
Associate Senior Editor

Please address questions and book requests to:
Silhouette Reader Service
U.S.: 3010 Walden Ave., P.O. Box 1325, Buffalo, NY 14269
Canadian: P.O. Box 609, Fort Erie, Ont. L2A 5X3

Linda Winstead Jones

One Major Distraction

INTIMATE MOMENTS™

Published by Silhouette Books

America's Publisher of Contemporary Romance

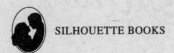

SILHOUETTE BOOKS

ISBN 0-373-27442-4

ONE MAJOR DISTRACTION

Visit Silhouette Books at www.eHarlequin.com

Printed in U.S.A.

LINDA WINSTEAD JONES

would rather write than do anything else. Since she cannot cook, gave up ironing many years ago, and finds cleaning the house a complete waste of time, she has plenty of time to devote to her obsession for writing. Occasionally she's tried to expand her horizons by taking classes. In the past she's taken instruction on yoga, French (a dismal failure), Chinese cooking, cake decorating (food-related classes are always a good choice, even for someone who can't cook), belly dancing (trust me, this was a long time ago) and, of course, creative writing.

She lives in Huntsville, Alabama, with her husband of more years than she's willing to admit and the youngest of their three sons.

She can be reached via www.eHarlequin.com or her own Web site www.lindawinsteadjones.com.

With love for brother Tom and Party Marty.
Wherever life takes you—rock on.

Chapter 1

Flynn Benning had been shot at a number of times, and he'd been stabbed, once. He'd staked out bad guys in freezing rain and hundred degree heat. He'd crawled through a swamp on his belly and swallowed more sand than he cared to remember. And this…this was the worst assignment he had ever taken, bar none.

Laura Stokes had her hand up again. That hand wasn't just lifted into the air, it waved and wiggled and the fingers danced. "Mr. Benning, Mr. Benning, Mr. Benning," she chirped when he didn't immediately acknowledge her raised hand. "This isn't the way Mr. Hill did it. Today is Thursday, so we should have a review of the vocabulary, and tomorrow we'll have the vocabulary test. That's the way he always did it."

Flynn glared, and the hand slowly drifted down. Laura Stokes was thirteen years old, redheaded, and wore glasses and braces. She was entering her gangly phase, and her voice was often whiny. Like now. He would feel sorry for her if she wasn't getting on his last nerve. Again.

Laura's more sedate schoolmate, Bev Martin, sat behind her and did her best to hide from Flynn and everyone else in the room. Bev leaned forward and whispered to Laura, no doubt advising her friend to back off before she got the entire class in trouble. Bev looked very much like Laura, in many ways. Her hair was a pale blond and she was taller, but they dressed the same and even wore similar small, gold-rimmed eyeglasses.

"I'm not Mr. Hill," Flynn said as he leaned casually against the desk he had been calling his own for two very long days. He raked his gaze quickly across the room, taking in the fourteen teenage girls who were enrolled in this history class. Many were more confident and poised than Laura and Bev, and a couple of the others always looked a little bit lost. For the duration of the current assignment he'd be teaching this class and three others. "Until Mr. Hill returns, we'll be doing things *my* way."

A twisted trail had brought Flynn and his team to this exclusive all-girls school in rural Georgia. In the past two weeks the headmistress, one sour Dr. Harriet Barber, had reported not one but two break-ins to the local sheriff's department. On the first occasion she'd found the window to her office open, when she was positive she'd locked it before retiring for the evening. The in-

vestigators had not taken that crime seriously, especially since nothing had been stolen. The second invasion had taken place in the same building. A window
had been broken. Again, nothing was taken, but by this
time Dr. Barber was livid. She'd insisted that a full investigation take place, including taking fingerprints.
Since she was tougher than the sheriff's investigators,
she got what she wanted.

More than one set of prints had been found, of
course, but after those who had access to the room were
cleared one set of fingerprints remained. They were entered into a database, searching for a match.

On Monday morning, a mere three days ago, a
match had been made. The fingerprints found on the
windowsill matched those found at the scene of a crime
that had taken place five years earlier, in Austin, Texas.
A robbery gone bad had left the man who'd surprised
the thief dead. All they had collected by way of evidence were the fingerprints and one blond hair. The
hair was from a female, and there was no way to be sure
if it had come from the thief or one of the victim's
many female friends. Just because they'd never been
able to match the hair to any known acquaintances
didn't mean it hadn't come from an innocent bystander,
so to speak.

The man who'd been killed had been very influential. Rumor was he had connections to the government.
Connections of the covert kind. The man had also been
a friend of Max Larkin's, and he was taking this personally. If the thief who'd killed Max's friend was here,

searching these old buildings for a treasure of some sort, Max wanted him caught.

Max Larkin worked in a consulting capacity for a government agency, and the Frances Teague Academy, an elite school for girls of middle and high school age, could be swarming with feds right now. Instead Max had hired the Benning Agency to get the job done. Max had hired the agency in the past, on more than one occasion. Their headquarters were tucked in back of a ratty old gas station in rural Alabama, but that didn't mean they weren't the best at what they did. Security, investigation, retrieval.

Hiring Flynn's agency gave Larkin some control over the situation. More than he would have had if this investigation became official. At the present time there wasn't enough evidence to interest the FBI—there was just enough to give Max hope that his friend's killer might be caught.

Max was too close to the situation to be involved. He hadn't taken it well when Flynn had told him he wasn't welcome here until the job was done.

Four members of the Benning team had arrived at the school Tuesday night, after dark. They had moved in as quietly and seamlessly as possible, and Dr. Barber was the only staff member who knew the reason for the intrusion.

Quinn Calhoun was now a soccer coach, Dante Mangino was a janitor and Sean Murphy had taken on the position of computer teacher. His boyish good looks had the older girls all agog. Flynn was teaching history. They had taken the places of four employees Max had been able to quickly clear of suspicion by comparing their fingerprints to those taken at the scene of the crime. In order to explain away the departure of four male staff members at the same time, they'd concocted a viral disease that would be laying the missing teachers, coach and janitor low for at least a few weeks. In truth, they were all relaxing quite comfortably in a safe house in South Florida, courtesy of Max Larkin. Not that they cared. South Florida in February was not a bad place to be. It beat a cold Georgia school filled with curious girls any day of the week.

Flynn's first instinct was to line up every employee on the grounds and take their fingerprints—along with a strand of hair from all the female employees, just in case. Max had nixed that idea at the outset. If the thief was watching, he'd be spooked by such an obvious inquiry, and that would never do.

Class was dismissed, the assignment for reading a chapter and writing a paper on the American Revolution made—even though, apparently, Mr. Hill would never do such a thing. Flynn would give the students a couple of days to work on their paper in class, which would save him from actually having to teach, at least for a while. After tomorrow, he'd have the weekend free. With any luck, they'd have Austin—the nickname they'd given the murdering thief—in custody by Monday. Not likely, but he could hope. Maybe Max would send him to Florida as a reward for a job so quickly and well done.

Not likely.

Flynn headed down the hall to the teachers' lounge. He had fifteen minutes between classes. If Austin was watching, he had to look like one of the guys. If Austin was already here, he needed to find the bastard before someone else got themselves killed. It was possible the thief had come and gone, but Max was willing to bet otherwise.

The Frances Teague Academy was situated on well-manicured grounds, with a number of ancient oak trees growing here and there. The place screamed of old money. It had once been a small private college, and that's what it looked like. For a period of several years, the place had stood empty. Had something of value been hidden here at that time? Maybe. Flynn hadn't been able to think of any other reason for Austin to be there.

Six redbrick buildings, all of them square and massive and studious-looking, made up the bulk of the campus. There was even ivy growing on the old walls. Two buildings were used for classes—one for girls of middle school age, one for high school. Two buildings were dormitories, for the girls who lived on campus and the female teachers. One, the smallest building, was housing for the male teachers and employees who opted not to live in town. The downstairs of that building sported a lounge of sorts, with an old television and a few mismatched chairs. Upstairs there were four small apartments, which were now occupied by the Benning agents.

The main building at the center of it all was where the administrative offices, the cafeteria and the gym were located. It was also the site of both break-ins.

The school's only security to this point had been a service from the small town nearby—two men who drove through slowly a few times a day. While it was tempting to ratchet up security, such a move would surely scare Austin away, if he was watching. Best to keep things as low-key as possible, until they had something concrete to work with.

The old buildings had been well maintained, but they were still old, and showed their age here and there. The room Flynn stepped into looked like teachers' lounges everywhere. There was a sagging couch someone had decided they no longer wanted, a round table with one leg that was slightly shorter than the others, a few mismatched chairs, a battered counter with a coffeepot and all the fixings, a narrow window that looked out over the grounds, and, of course, a few teachers.

A few suspects? Flynn didn't even know with any certainty that they were looking for a man. They had assumed the thief and killer was a man, they referred to Austin as "he." But that wasn't necessarily the case. For all they knew, the blond hair had come from Austin. Was she here right now, searching for some sort of valuable hidden in the main building? Something worth spending months here to find? There were a handful of teachers who were new to the school this year, who could have come in for the express purpose of gaining access to the school. Two of them were in this room.

Serena Loomis was a math teacher, and she looked the part. Her dark hair was very short, her glasses were small and black-rimmed and she was always dressed very precisely, in tailored shirts and neatly pressed slacks. The woman looked like she didn't ever wrinkle. Or smile. Her records said she was thirty-six, and she looked to be that age, or close to it.

Stephanie McCabe was a polar opposite from the math teacher. She taught English and was irritatingly bubbly. According to her file she was twenty-nine. She was pretty, blond and wore froufrou dresses and too much makeup. She also sold makeup, as a sideline, and had already tried to sell Flynn skin care products made especially for men. She hadn't taken kindly to his response that where he was from skin care products for men were called *soap*.

Both women were new faculty members, which had moved them to the top of Flynn's short list of suspects. Even though Loomis looked tough, neither of them actually looked like they were capable of murder, but you could never tell. Getting prints from Loomis and McCabe should be easy enough, but the move had to be subtle. No one had ever accused Flynn Benning of being subtle. He eyed their coffee mugs and wondered if it would be possible to scoop them up and retrieve usable prints.

As he crossed to room, Loomis nodded to him. McCabe's smile died, and she made a dismissive huffing noise. Harry Kaylor, biology teacher, hovered over the almost empty coffeepot. His greeting was even less enthusiastic than McCabe's. Kaylor was not one of Flynn's prime suspects. He was getting close to retirement—had in fact passed retirement age—and had been at this school for more than twelve years. Unfortunately, none of the handful of male employees had been here less than four years, which all but eliminated them from suspicion.

It was just as possible, perhaps more likely, that Austin was living in town, watching and waiting for the right opportunity to break into the main building once again. All Flynn had to do was find out what he was searching for. And wait.

The door behind Flynn swung open, and a woman bearing a tray of cookies stormed in. She wore a shapeless white uniform, comfortable shoes and no makeup, and still she caught Flynn's eye. There was something very pretty about the curve of her cheek and the color of her skin. Auburn hair, thick and wavy, had been caught in a ponytail, and something about it just begged to be set free. Made Flynn's fingers itch.

"I baked more cookies than we need for lunch," she said, her Southern accent soft but unmistakable, "and I thought y'all might like to help me finish them off."

The response she received was much warmer than the one Flynn had gotten when he'd walked in. Of course, he hadn't brought cookies. He also wasn't nearly so pretty. The woman skirted past Flynn and headed for the counter by the coffeepot, where she deposited the sweets. Without asking, she took out the old filter and wet grounds and began to make a fresh pot.

"Bless you," Kaylor said. "Your coffee is always so much better than mine. I'm not sure why."

"I have the magic touch," the woman teased.

She glanced over her shoulder to Flynn, and her smile dimmed. They hadn't officially met, but he had noticed her in the cafeteria last night, dishing up grilled chicken breasts and steamed broccoli and rice. Last night her auburn hair had been caught in a hairnet that had not been particularly flattering. He liked the ponytail better.

When Dr. Barber had presented Flynn with a roster of the employees who had arrived in the fall, there hadn't been any cafeteria personnel listed. Still, it wouldn't hurt to be thorough.

He stepped forward and offered his hand. "Flynn Benning. I just started teaching here yesterday. History."

She continued to make coffee, ignoring his offered hand. "Tess Stafford."

"Tess works in the dining hall," Kaylor said unnecessarily, when it became clear that Tess didn't intend to offer any more information about herself. "She takes good care of us, and brings us cookies and brownies and such, now and then."

Flynn glanced down at the heart-shaped cookies on the platter by the coffeepot. Kaylor had already grabbed one, and Loomis and McCabe were both headed this way. "Hearts?"

"It is Valentine's Day," Stephanie McCabe said as she reached past Tess Stafford and grabbed one of the pink-iced cookies.

"Is it?" Flynn asked. "I hadn't realized."

Loomis snorted as she reclaimed her seat. "Don't you watch television, Mr. Benning? Or listen to the radio? Or read the newspaper?"

"I don't watch much television," he admitted. And when it came to the newspaper, he usually read the first page and skimmed the rest.

Stephanie remained near the counter, standing right next to Tess Stafford. "When are you going to let me give you that makeover?" she asked, her eyes on the cafeteria lady's face. "You have such good bone structure and such excellent skin tone, if you'd just get started with a good, daily skin care regimen…"

"I really don't have time," Stafford said as she finished with the coffeemaker and backed away. She came inches from running into Flynn. He did a quick recon. Age: probably mid-thirties. Height: five foot five inches, or thereabouts. Physical condition: above average. There were nicely sculpted muscles in her upper arms, and underneath that baggy white uniform she looked to be in excellent shape. Socially: awkward, cautious. She definitely hadn't been eager to make friends with him.

Stafford scooped up the dirty mugs, much to Flynn's dismay, and left the lounge with an awkward wave for the other teachers and the instruction to make do with the foam cups until she got the mugs washed and returned to the lounge. Tempted as Flynn was to tackle her and snag the fingerprinted crockery, he dismissed the idea. There would be other chances.

He headed for the coffeepot and the cookies. "She seems to know her way around the school pretty well. How long has she been here?"

"This is her first full year," Kaylor said. "She settled

in real nice, though, so it seems like she's been here a lot longer."

"Does she live on campus?" Some teachers and other personnel did. Others didn't.

"She and another cafeteria worker have rooms on the second floor of the main building. The part-timers live in town, but Tess and Mary Jo have to start so early and work so late, it just makes sense for them to be close by the dining hall."

"Makes sense." Flynn took a bite of the Valentines' Day cookie. His instincts where people were concerned were highly tuned, and he always listened to them. Tess Stafford had the look of a woman who was hiding something. Something big, something she didn't want him to uncover. She put his senses on alert in a way the other women—who made more viable suspects—didn't.

In preparing for this job, Flynn had seen crime scene photos of the murder in Austin. He wanted to believe it was unlikely a woman could commit such a brutal and bloody murder, but he had learned never to be surprised. Accepting that lesson had made life so much easier.

Tess had a good grip on the mugs, grasping them all by the handles as she hurried toward the main building. She thought, more than once, that she should've grabbed her sweater before heading out to deliver cookies. Some days the cold weather took her by surprise. In just a few weeks, the spring warmth would move in and everything would change. For now, there were cold days and colder nights.

The new history teacher set her teeth on edge, and

she wasn't sure why. He was extremely nice-looking, with very short blond hair, a chiseled jaw and a fit body. He had to be six foot two, at least, with wide shoulders and long legs and more than his share of muscle. He was old enough to be interesting, but was young enough to be, well, interesting. Late thirties maybe, judging by the lines around his eyes. He didn't exactly look uncomfortable in his khakis and button-up shirt, so why did she get the feeling that the casual but professional outfit was not his usual garb? Maybe because he wasn't built anything like the other male teachers around here. He didn't look like any teacher she had ever known, here or in her own academic years.

Looks aside, he was undoubtedly one of *those guys*—those macho men who thought they could do anything and everything better than anyone else, who always felt compelled to fix everything that was broken, who expected women to fall at their feet if they smiled at them, who expected that everything in life would always go their way.

She'd had her fill of those guys.

In addition to his size and his build and his chiseled jaw, Benning also had great blue eyes that were too curious for Tess's liking. She didn't need curious at this point in her life. If anyone found out who she was and why she was here…

Before she reached the main building, something caught Tess's eye and she stopped. Out by the soccer field, the new coach was talking with great animation to the new janitor. The back of her neck prickled, and it had nothing to do with the cool weather. Neither of them were quite right for their new jobs. Coach Calhoun was tough as old leather, even though he was years younger than Benning. His eyes were too sharp for a girls' soccer coach, and he moved too quickly and precisely. He could be an athlete himself. A job as coach at a small all-girls' school shouldn't attract this type of man, and yet here he was.

The new janitor was definitely out of place here. He had long, thick dark hair, intelligent dark eyes and a body that would not quit. He also had a number of tattoos on his person, most of which she could only see a corner or an edge of. One just barely peeking over his collar, another on his forearm. Both were mostly hidden by an unflattering gray uniform. From what Tess knew of Dr. Barber, the woman would rather clean the place herself than hire a man who looked like this one. Didn't make any sense at all.

Sean Murphy had come to work here at the same time as the other three. If not for that fact, she might not think him at all out of place. He was almost pretty, and did not have the toughness of the other three. He smiled often, unlike the others, and he actually looked like a computer nerd. A pretty computer nerd, but still…a nerd. But the fact that he had come in at the same time, combined with the fact that she'd seen Murphy talking to Benning last night after supper, raised her suspicions.

Something was up. She wasn't sure what, exactly, but she didn't like it. First the break-ins, where nothing was taken, and now this testosterone invasion.

From the soccer field, two heads lifted at once and

turned her way. The two men were too far for her to see those eyes to know if they were really looking at her, and still she felt a chill. She rubbed her arms and started walking toward the main building once again.

As long as they weren't here for her—and how could they be?—she didn't care what they were up to.

Benning and his team were closed up in one small apartment—his—for the moment. No wonder Kaylor and most of the other teachers opted to live in town. These rooms assigned to the teachers were small— one-bedroom apartments with a sad little kitchenette in the main room and a very small bedroom attached. The bathroom was the size of a postage stamp.

"We need to gather as much info as we can as quickly as possible so we can finish this up and get out of here. We don't know anything concrete about Austin, so we're taking nothing for granted. Not even the suppo- sition that he's a man."

"Do you know something we don't?" Cal asked sharply. Cal would prefer to be searching for his sister Kelly. For the moment he was allowing the newly mar- ried Sadie Harlow, Flynn's only female agent, to work that cold and frustrating case.

"No, and that's just the point. We don't have nearly enough information about Austin. Take nothing for granted. It's possible the person we're looking for— male or female—is right here searching for something. We need to accomplish two things right off the bat. We need to fit in as if we've been here a long while, so as not to raise any suspicions. If Austin has been watching from a distance, maybe he won't notice that some of the faces have changed. If we moved in here with an openly armed team, he'd see and we'd lose him for sure. Make friends, do your jobs and keep your eyes open."

"Number two?" Dante prompted.

"There's something here Austin wants. Something valuable. If he hasn't already found what he came here for, then we need to find it first. We get started with the who. Who doesn't belong here? Who's not quite right? Murphy," Flynn snapped, "you take McCabe."

Murphy groaned, saying nothing until Cal nudged him with an elbow. Then he laughed and said, "She says I'm a metrosexual. I don't know what that is, but even though it has "sexual" in it, I don't think it's a good thing."

"It means you'll let her give you a facial," Dante said with a laugh.

Flynn turned to Dante. "You get Loomis."

The laugh died quickly. "The math teacher?"

"Yeah."

"But…"

"But what?"

"She's not blond, she's flat-chested and I'm not a hundred percent certain she's, you know, playing for the right team."

"I caught her staring at your ass this afternoon when you were mopping the hallway so I don't think you have to worry about what team she plays on."

Dante grumbled, but not much.

"I'm not asking you to sleep with her," Flynn said

with a snort. "Just get friendly. Suck it up and do your job." He turned to Cal while Dante mumbled. "You get Tess Stafford. I don't have a lot of information on her yet. Dr. Barber apparently didn't think to include her in the original list, since she lives in the main building and has no need to break in. Lucky is digging up what he can on her. She works in the cafeteria and—"

"No way," Cal said, lifting his left hand to wag the ring finger and the attached gold band.

"This is work, Calhoun," Flynn said sharply. "I'm not asking you to marry the woman. Just make friends. What's the matter with you guys?" He looked from one agent to the next. It was bad enough that Lucky Santana had all but refused to participate in the undercover element of this operation. Not that Lucky would fit in here. He didn't have the qualifications to be a substitute teacher, like Flynn and Murphy did, and he'd never pass for a janitor or a soccer coach. Besides, Lucky was still ticked off about losing his partner Sadie to marriage, and he was a bear to work with these days. He was at the home office in Alabama, handling research and moping.

This was a tough job for Flynn, for reasons he chose not to share with his employees, but from their standpoint this should be a walk in the park. "This is the easiest freakin' job you've ever had and you're whining like a bunch of pansies."

"Okay," Cal said in a calm voice. "You call Livvie and tell her what I'm doing on this job besides coaching soccer, and we'll see how it goes."

"I'm not afraid of your wife," Flynn said darkly.

"What about her uncle, who seems determined that her every wish should be granted?"

True, Max Larkin could be trouble. "Fine," Flynn growled. "You coach soccer and call your wife every night like a good boy, and I'll take Stafford."

Which wouldn't exactly be a chore, as long as she didn't turn out to be a cold-blooded killer.

Flynn smiled at Cal. "You can take Leon Toller."

"The weirdo art teacher who likes to walk around talking to himself?"

"You prove Toller's not Austin, and I'll charm the cafeteria lady."

Words he'd never thought to speak, or even to imagine.

"Yes, Major," Cal said without emotion.

"I'm not a major anymore, Calhoun," Flynn replied. Cal knew that. They all did. He'd been retired from the Marines for years.

This job was unlike any other he had ever participated in. He and his team usually went in with guns blazing. They didn't pretend; they didn't finesse. And yet here they were, undercover in a sea of little girls and academics, at Max Larkin's request.

No doubt about it; he'd rather face a firefight any day.

Patience was not Dale's strong suit, but that's what this job called for. Patience. There was some pride in being adaptable to each situation, and that was soothing, in an odd sort of way.

At night this all-girl's school possessed an unexpected serenity. The bustling of the day was over, the students and the teachers had retired for the evening and the grounds were silent. Warm light spilled through dormitory windows, while others remained dark. The thick Georgia air spread over the campus like a blanket. Even in the wintertime, it was humid here. The cold cut to the bone, some nights.

Fortunately these nighttime excursions were an infrequent requirement. Serenity aside, the cold was something jarring. Cancún was much nicer this time of year, and as soon as this job was finished that destination would call. This assignment paid nicely, enough to hide away quietly for a long time to come. Thinking of warm beaches almost took away the winter chill. Almost.

Weather was a small quandary, comparatively speaking. There had been a few strange faces on the campus today. After months of routine and monotony, *strange* was startling and unwelcomed. There was, perhaps, a logical explanation, but still, it was disturbing. Dale had never cared for being disturbed. Routine was much more soothing.

Eyes closed, Dale thought of Cancún and took a deep breath of the cold, humid air. In that cold air was a new scent, a touch of spring. And with the coming of spring came the end of this well-planned job. Not tonight, not tomorrow…but soon.

Chapter 2

"That looks good," Benning said, flashing one of those charming smiles mcn used when they thought they were being, well, charming. "Did you make it yourself?"

Tess shook her head. "No. Mary Jo made the meatloaf." Mary Jo stood at the head of the line, passing out salad. She was a very nice, bone-thin grandmother who had a room next to Tess's but was only there during the week. On the weekends, she stayed with her son and grandkids who lived in town, and came in to work for a few hours each day.

Mary Jo and Tess were the only full-time cafeteria employees, and the only ones who worked the supper shift. They were especially busy in the evenings, which meant that she did not have time to entertain the new guy, or anyone else.

"Oh." The big man who had parked himself in front of her looked almost disappointed. "What did you make?"

"You're holding up the line," she snapped.

"So answer my question and I'll move on."

"I made the scalloped potatoes and the apple pie," Tess said through clenched teeth.

"They both look great." Benning did his best to lean over the counter. He was so darn big he could almost do just that. "So, why don't you have a date for Valentine's Day?"

His bold question startled her. It crossed the line between friendly and flirting, and to be honest she didn't have time for either. Finally Tess answered, "What makes you think I don't have a late date?"

"Do you?"

With a wave of her hand, she shooed him down the line. "I'd like to get these girls fed, if you don't mind."

He grudgingly moved along, muttering something about her late date, and Tess turned her attention to the kids who were waiting in line for their supper. Not all the students lived on campus, but those who did were in this cafeteria for three meals a day. They were good girls, for the most part, and she liked her job more than she'd ever imagined she would. Some days it took her back to her own days in school. She'd been so naive, just like so many of these girls. But it had been a special time, one she remembered with fondness, for the most part.

Thirteen-year-old Laura came along just minutes behind Benning. She and her friend Bev were the last students in line, as usual, and for them Tess had a wide and real smile.

"Cute top," Tess said, nodding to the striped sweater Laura wore.

"Thanks." Laura squirmed as if the compliment made her uncomfortable. "My dad sent it to me last week."

"It looks nice and warm, and that green is your color."

Laura wrinkled her nose. She definitely did not like talking about herself.

"And Bev, you look fabulous in blue. It brings out your eyes."

Bev gave in to an odd sort of smile, but it didn't last.

"I saw you talking to Mr. Benning," Laura said. "Do you like him, or something?"

"No," Tess answered precisely. "I do *not* like him. In fact, the man really gets on my nerves."

"He gets on my nerves, too," Laura said.

"He's a little scary," Bev said in a low voice Tess had to strain to hear.

"He doesn't do things the way Mr. Hill did," Laura said in a slightly louder voice. The changes in her history class obviously upset her. Laura didn't like change. And at thirteen, everything was changing, or soon would.

"Maybe Mr. Hill will have a quick recovery and be back in class before you know it," Tess said optimistically.

"I hope so," Laura said as she continued down the line.

"Me, too," Bev said, cutting her eyes to Tess and trying that uncertain smile once again.

Tess's smile died as the girls headed for a table in the dining hall. Laura and Bev were both awkward, but then they were at an awkward age. Neither of the girls thought they were pretty, but they would be, as soon as they grew into themselves and gained some confidence. She saw them glance at the table where the more popular girls sat, giggling and whispering and posing. They were either older than Laura and Bev, or else they had matured at an earlier age. There was no awkwardness at that table of pretty, self-assured girls.

Tess often found herself trying to help the girls in this school, above and beyond the duties of a cook. So many of them had been shuffled off because their parents didn't have time for them, or because divorce had split up the family and boarding school seemed a safe and easy alternative. They all came from money, or else they wouldn't be here; that new sweater Laura was wearing probably cost more than a week's salary for Tess.

"More?"

Tess's head snapped around to find that Flynn Benning was back and offering his plate for a refill of scalloped potatoes. The fact that he'd surprised her counted against him. Had he noticed her staring at Laura and Bev?

No, he was much too self-absorbed to notice any such thing. That grin of his was wicked and just short of smarmy. If he winked at her, she was going to throw the potatoes at him. How would he look *wearing* his second helping? He didn't wink, and she scooped up enough scalloped potatoes for four men his size and slopped them into his plate with a twist of her wrist. "How's that?"

"Thank you," he said. "There's just something extra special about these potatoes. I'm not sure what it is."

Tess rolled her eyes and turned away, but not before she caught a glimpse of something unexpected in Benning's blue eyes.

Suspicion.

He was a good judge of character, he trusted his instincts, and something about Tess Stafford raised more than one alarm. She was too savvy to be working as a cafeteria cook, server and dishwasher in a private school. In his day they had been called lunchroom ladies, and none of them had looked anything like Tess Stafford. She didn't make much money here, the living quarters left a lot to be desired and making heart-shaped cookies for little girls and teachers might be fulfilling in some basic womanly way, but it definitely wasn't challenging.

Not for the first time, Flynn wondered what the hell he was doing here. Only for Max would he put himself in this situation. Sadie Harlow—Sadie McCain, now, Flynn reminded himself—would be perfect for this assignment. It would be much easier for her to work her way into the closed circle of women employees without rousing suspicion. But Sadie had gone and gotten herself pregnant, and for some reason her husband, Truman McCain, had a problem with letting her hunt down murdering thieves in her current condition. Flynn almost snorted just thinking about it. He'd never imagined that anyone could forbid Sadie to do anything. Just as well.

If she was here and pregnant, he'd have to worry about her himself. Besides, anything Sadie could do, he could do. How much of a challenge could Tess Stafford, who made heart-shaped cookies and served up three meals a day, be?

Tess was presently wiping down tables in a deserted dining hall. The students and the teachers who lived on campus had all headed for their dorms, and the other woman who worked in the cafeteria had retired for the night. Stafford was lost in thought as she wiped down a table where some of the messier girls had eaten supper.

"Need any help?"

Her head snapped up at his softly spoken question, and she stopped wiping. "What do you want?"

He shrugged his shoulders. "There's not much to do in my room. I thought I'd help you out here so you can get to your late date. We wouldn't want you to be tardy."

She started scrubbing again, harder this time. "Okay, let's get something straight, Mr. Benning. Just because I work in an all-girls' school, doesn't mean I'm desperate for a man to come along and charm me out of my orthopedic shoes. I'm not desperate for anything. I'm not looking for a man, and if I were it wouldn't be you because you're not my type."

"Does that mean there's no late date?"

"No," she finally admitted, "there's no late date. Not only that, I don't want a date, late or otherwise."

Tess Stafford was pretty and she knew how to stand up for herself, and she was also angry. A man was the cause, most likely. Wasn't that always the story? It was like some sad country song. A good-for-nothing fella had broken her heart and stolen her life savings, and run off in the night with her dog and her pickup truck.

Charming her was going to be more difficult than he'd imagined.

"Okay, you don't want a date, you don't need a man. How about a friend? Got more of those than you need?"

Tess stopped wiping, but kept her eyes on the table. Had he touched a chord with her? Anger just beneath the surface aside, she seemed to be a nice person. The others who worked here liked her, but she didn't let anyone get too close. He could see that from here. Hell, he'd seen it at first glance.

"You can start by calling me Flynn," he said. "I get enough Mr. Benning during the day. Usually like this." He raised his hand and waggled his fingers, "Mr. Benning, Mr. Benning, Mr. Benning."

He saw the start of a reluctant smile. It just barely turned up the corners of Tess's nicely wide mouth. "Kids can be relentless." She began wiping again, slower this time.

"Tell me about it," he said, leaning against the doorjamb and watching her work. Relaxed this way, she was very pretty. Very out of place in this stark room. "I'll make you a deal. I'll help you clean, and then over leftover apple pie and some of your fabulous coffee, you can tell me all about the other people who work here. It's tough being the new guy in town."

She lifted her head and looked him square in the eye, as if trying to judge his intentions. "Sure," she finally said. "Why not?"

* * *

Tess told herself that if she could figure out why Flynn Benning was so curious, if she could reassure herself that his being here had nothing to do with her, it would be worth spending a little extra time in his company.

Over coffee and apple pie, they started an awkward conversation. She had never been one to make friends easily, and he didn't strike her as the gregarious type. Confident, yes. Gregarious, never.

She told Flynn what she knew of some of the teachers he'd be working alongside, general information that he could have gotten anywhere, and he listened carefully. Maybe too carefully, for someone who was a sub who wouldn't be here very long. He was either way too interested in the goings-on at the Frances Teague Academy, or else he was way too interested in her.

"You'll only be working here until Scott Hill is better, right?" she asked.

"That's right."

"Where do you usually teach?"

It was a perfectly natural question to ask a new teacher, but it looked as if he bristled a little. "I used to teach at a military school south of Atlanta."

Military school. *That* she could see. The size, the bearing, the way he took charge of a room just by walking through the door. Military. "What happened?" she asked. "Why aren't you teaching there this year?"

For a moment, she thought he wasn't going to answer. His shoulders squared, his spine straightened, and those eyes…the blue was almost electric.

"A new administrator comes in and decides she wants things done her way," he finally said. "We were supposed to be sensitive and new-agey and it was all crap."

Tess smiled, she could see it so well. "You told her so in just those words, didn't you?"

"Yeah," he answered, visibly calmer and almost sheepish. "Now here I am teaching at an all-girls school, which is ironic, I suppose. I look at some of these girls the wrong way, and I swear they're about to burst into tears. I don't do tears."

She laughed out loud, surprising him and herself.

"It's not funny," he said, almost seriously.

"It is, actually," she answered.

"Well, I probably won't be here more than a couple of weeks. That's what I was told, anyway. If I can get through this assignment without making any of the little girls cry, I'll be fine."

Well, crap. She liked him. The fact that he would stand up to an administrator who wanted to run things in a way he didn't care for was one thing. But he was actually worried about making little girls cry. There was something unexpected about that, coming from a big man who was undeniably gruff.

Her pie was gone, her coffee cup almost empty. She'd told Flynn everything she could think of, about the faculty and staff he'd be dealing with in his time here. And she wasn't quite ready to leave. Evenings were the toughest part of the day, for her. Alone in her apartment above stairs, the hours went by too slowly, and her imagination ran wild. She thought about getting caught, about losing everything she'd worked for.

But this was nice. She liked Benning, he apparently liked her, and even though it could never go anywhere it was nice to have someone to talk to. A friend, he said.

"So, Flynn. That's an unusual name. Is it a family name?"

He grunted slightly and took a big bite of pie. The last bite. She waited patiently while he finished it off with a swig of black coffee. "Not a family name," he finally said. "As a matter of fact, I was suppose to be named John William Benning III, but my mother had other ideas."

"So, where does the Flynn come from?"

He pushed his plate and cup aside and leaned onto the table. He'd rolled his sleeves up, displaying utterly masculine forearms. She really, really wanted to touch them, just for a moment, but of course she didn't.

"That's enough about me," he said. "What's a woman like you doing working in a cafeteria? You're smart, you're pretty, you're energetic and everyone likes you. So, why aren't you married and raising a half dozen kids, or running a corporation, or teaching home economics or…"

Tess's smile died. The man was way too curious about her. She grabbed the dirty dishes and stood, keeping her gaze on the last little bit of coffee that was left in the bottom of Flynn's mug. "It's getting late," she said. "And I have to be up early in the morning to make biscuits."

"I didn't mean to—"

"You didn't do anything," she interrupted. "I just didn't realize how late it was. The time got away from me."

A very large, very warm hand shot out and gripped her wrist, and for a moment she was frozen. Flynn's fingers were like a warm, soft vise. An unexpected electricity worked through her body. It had been a long time since she'd allowed any man to touch her, even in such a simple way.

It was so stupid, to stand here and imagine what it would be like to lay her fingers on that hard forearm, or fix the little crinkle in his collar, or run her palm against his short, fair hair. There wasn't time for any of that in her life…not today, and not tomorrow. Maybe never.

"I'm sorry," he said, letting his hand fall away. "I didn't mean to push. Friends don't push."

Maybe he would be smart and not push now, as she hurried toward the kitchen. "I'll see you in the morning," she called back without looking over her shoulder. "Do me a favor and make sure the door is locked when you leave?"

"Sure," he said softly as he left the dining hall. "I'll double check to be certain the building is secure."

Somehow that assurance made her feel a little better, even as she climbed the stairs to her little apartment.

Flynn didn't rush back to his quarters in the men's dormitory. The night was cold, the air downright icy, and yet the chill didn't bother him at all.

Tess Stafford didn't belong here, not in the cafeteria,

anyway. She was hiding something, and he wanted to know what it was. Was she a natural blonde who hid her true colors under auburn hair color? Could someone who lied so badly be Austin? Could someone who didn't dare look a man in the eye while she made a hasty escape kill a man for a painting and a handful of very nice jewelry? Could a woman who trembled at the innocent touch of a hand on her wrist be here planning another crime?

He didn't think so, and Dr. Barber's argument that she had no need to break into the building where she lived was valid enough. But until Lucky came back with a report that cleared her, he compared her fingerprints to Austin's and he got hold of a strand of hair to compare to the one taken from the scene of the crime in Texas, Tess Stafford would remain on Flynn's list of suspects. He couldn't take her off the list just because he—unexpectedly and against his better judgment—wanted to sleep with her.

Tess might not be Austin, but she was hiding something. Something big. Something that kept her here.

There was to be a meeting in his room at ten o'clock—fifteen minutes—and he didn't feel compelled to hurry. Instead he looked around, studying the darkened buildings where classes would resume in the morning and the dormitories where students and female teachers were either already asleep or getting ready for bed. Some of them would be asleep by now, he imagined. The windows that were still lit up were probably rooms of the teachers and the older girls.

He hadn't been lying when he'd told Tess that he was

terrified of making the girls cry. Most everything else had been pure fabrication. The military school, the background that had been manufactured for this assignment, it was all false. But he was truly terrified of coming face-to-face with a sobbing teenage girl.

His own little girl would be fourteen, if she'd lived. Denise would be thirty-eight. There were days when it seemed like ages ago that he'd buried his wife and daughter, and there were other days when it seemed like yesterday. His job didn't normally require him to face his past. He'd grieved, and then he'd moved on as best he could. He hadn't forgotten, but he had relegated that long-ago pain to a safe and remote place. These past two days had brought it all a little closer than he cared for. All these little girls reminded him too sharply of the one he'd lost.

All the more reason to find Austin and get out of here ASAP.

Cal and Murphy were right on time for the meeting, but Dante was running late. Flynn was in no mood for waiting, but he hated having to do anything twice. The three of them made themselves comfortable, Cal and Murphy on the couch, Flynn in a sagging chair.

Cal thought Leon Toller was just a sad, weird little man who didn't have many friends because he spent most of his time in his own world. He was divorced, no surprise, and had three boys he didn't see very often. That matched the info they had on him, so far. Cal had snagged a porcelain doodad from the man's class, and it was already on the way to Max for fingerprint comparison.

While Cal was talking Murphy kept rubbing his cheek, until Flynn finally snapped. "What's wrong with your face?"

"Stephanie gave me a facial. My skin feels different. It's smooth."

Cal started to laugh, then noted that Flynn was not amused and went silent.

"A facial," Flynn repeated in a low voice.

"Yeah. It's the only way I could, you know…"

"Get into her pants?" Cal asked when Murphy faltered.

"No," Murphy said. "She's not that kind of girl. She's very passionate about her English classes and this line of makeup and skin-care products she sells. Most of it's all natural. The makeup, not the English classes. She gave me a sample of a skin cream for men. It smells pretty good."

"You *are* a metrosexual," Cal said.

Murphy muttered beneath his breath, "I still don't know what that means."

Dante arrived, to Flynn's great relief, slightly red-faced and not his usual cool self.

"Where the hell have you been?" Flynn asked.

Dante walked into the room, but didn't sit. Instead, he paced. "The math teacher is a freak."

Cal and Murphy both leaned forward, unduly interested. "In what way?" Cal asked. "She has six toes on one foot? She used to work at a sideshow as the bearded lady? What?"

"Not a freak in a bad way," Dante said. "She's aggressive. She knows what she wants and she goes for it.

Man, does she go for it. I thought math teachers were supposed to be shy and repressed, but not Serena Loomis. No, there's nothing repressed about her. Man, I'm sorry I'm late, but I didn't think she was going to let me *go*."

"You've been in her room all this time?" Murphy asked.

Dante shook his head. "No. She was afraid one of the students would see me going to her room, or leaving. There's a gardener's shed out back, so we went there. If Austin is a man, it's not Serena Loomis. She's, uh, also not blond. Natural brunette."

Flynn leaned back in his chair, on edge and impatient. "Murphy is a woman and Mangino got laid," he said sharply. "Did we manage to gather any other useful information tonight?"

A breathless Dante nodded his head. "Maybe. Serena mentioned that there's a parents' weekend coming up in two weeks," he said. "Considering how much it costs to attend this school, we have to look at every parent who's going to be here that weekend as a potential target. Maybe what Austin wants to steal isn't here, but will be. He took jewels before."

"Killed for 'em," Cal added.

Dante dismissed his momentous evening and turned his attention to the matter at hand. "We're talking about a one-day event, which means anything of value will be in the possession of a parent. That means we're looking at armed robbery, not simple theft."

With that bit of information, the mood in the room changed. Back to business; they didn't have time to spare.

Flynn nodded to Murphy. "I'll need a list of all those parents. Dr. Barber will cooperate, I'm sure, but she has been less than thorough." First Tess was left off the list of new employees, and now this. Surely she knew that the parents' weekend would be of interest.

Then again, they hadn't told her everything, either.

"I want to go outside the school for information, as well. I want everything."

Murphy left the couch. "You got it." Since their computer genius was a night owl, he'd probably have something substantial to report by morning. Cal promised to help, after he called his wife again, and Dante headed for his room, apparently for some well-deserved rest.

When they were all gone, Flynn went to the window to look over the campus. Crap. He wanted to be out of here ASAP, but this was a deadline he could do without. If he didn't find Austin in the next two weeks, he'd have a campus brimming with potential victims. He could insist that the parents' weekend be canceled, and Max could make it happen, but if they did that Austin would be spooked and might not resurface for years.

Besides, there was no guarantee that the target was among the parents. All they knew with any certainty was that Austin had been here.

He tried to imagine Tess Stafford planning to rob one or more of the parents, in between baking cookies and brewing coffee and giving the most inept of the girls a little extra smile and conversation. And he couldn't make it work.

But he knew too well that didn't mean Tess Stafford wasn't the one he was looking for.

"Time for bed," Truman said gently. "You need your sleep."

Sadie looked away from the computer screen long enough to smile widely at her husband. He had always been overly protective, but now that she was pregnant he was downright possessive.

A part of her actually liked it.

"I think I found her."

Truman cocked his head and smiled at her. Sometimes just looking at him still made her heart go *thump*. "She'll still be there come morning."

"Maybe," Sadie muttered. Kelly Calhoun never stayed in one place very long, but she did have a tendency to come back to the South on a regular basis. "I don't want to lose her again."

Truman laid his hands on her shoulders and massaged lightly. "Are you going to call Cal and tell him?"

Sadie shook her head as she typed the last of the e-mail message to the private eye who'd found Kelly. Maybe. "No. I don't want to get his hopes up and then come up empty-handed again. He's been through that too many times."

Her husband bent down and kissed her cheek. "You're a good friend," he said. "And a good wife," His hand settled over her stomach. "And a good mother."

Sadie smiled at the computer screen. Once she found Kelly for Cal, she was going to take some serious time off. Like maybe until the last of the kids started school. She'd never imagined she could feel this way.

"So," Truman said, leaning against her and hanging on lightly. "Where is she this time?"

"Close," she answered, then she finished her e-mail and glanced up. "Kelly's back in Georgia."

Chapter 3

Saturdays were nice on campus, even when it was cold. Peaceful. Quiet, in a way that touched the soul. On most Saturday mornings and many weekday afternoons, if it wasn't too cold, Tess took a turn or two around the nature trail that wound through pine trees and old oaks and thick underbrush. The path itself, which circled around the soccer field and cleared the thick growth on the side nearest the parking lot, was kept clear of debris and poison ivy by the landscaping crew that came in once a week. The kids walked and ran on this trail, in their spare time or as part of their physical education class. And still, when she walked the path alone it felt as if no one else ever came here. The wild growth and the whisper of trees was miles away from the sparkling appliances of the massive kitchen.

Tess walked briskly around the path to stay warm, her eyes on the soccer field where one of the teams was practicing. It was the middle school team, she knew. The Ladybugs. Laura and Bev were on the team, though from what she'd seen in weeks past they didn't get to play much. Neither of them was athletic enough to get a lot of playing time. Of course, the entire team was less than athletically stellar. Maybe they'd improve before the season started, but from what she'd heard that wasn't likely. The soccer teams usually both finished last or near last in their divisions. Coach West had been very laid-back, and if his complacence had been a part of his coaching style she could see why the teams hadn't done well.

Coach Calhoun wasn't at all laid-back. He yelled at the girls when they made a mistake, and there had been one or two times when she'd been sure he was literally pulling out his hair. It was early in the soccer year, and some of the newer girls had a tendency to run in the wrong direction or use their hands when they shouldn't. As one of the girls used a hand to deflect a ball, Calhoun ran across the field to yell at her, up close and personal.

Quinn Calhoun was as out of place at this all-girls' school as Flynn Benning. Maybe he'd been fired from the same military school at which Flynn had once taught. Military certainly described them both, though neither Dante Mangino nor Sean Murphy fell into that category. And still…she was sometimes sure the four of them were up to something. Then again, her imagination had gotten the best of her in the past, and here she was again—imagining trouble.

She hadn't come out here to think about Flynn! In fact, she was here in part to get him out of her mind. Tess turned her attention to the soccer field, as she took a turn in the path. Laura had her hair up in a curly ponytail this morning, and Bev's was styled much the same, though her ponytail was straight and sleek. Those two stuck together, whenever they could. That was a good thing. Laura needed a good friend. She'd heard enough from Laura to know that her sorry excuse for a father hadn't been much of a friend to her, and apparently that new stepmother of hers didn't care to spend any more time with the kid than she had to. Still, Laura *was* thirteen, so it was possible her observations were colored by teenage angst. Tess wanted to see for herself what kind of father Jack Stokes was.

Tess had already begun to worry about the parents' weekend coming up. Two weeks from today, the campus would be swarming with mothers and fathers anxious to explore the school and meet everyone. Would cafeteria personnel be included in that list? Would Jack even bother to come? And if he did, was it possible that he wouldn't even recognize her after all this time? Thirteen years was such a long time, and she'd changed. She'd changed very much.

Tess walked briskly, keeping up the pretense of getting her morning exercise. But as often as she could, she watched her daughter.

Jack had stolen her baby from her, and if she could find a way to steal her daughter back without breaking the girl's heart she would. She hadn't been able to think of a way to reclaim Laura without turning the girl's world upside down and inside out, so she watched when she could, and tried to be a friend, and cried herself to sleep at night when it seemed like she would never find a way to fix everything in her life that was broken....

"Hey, Red."

Speaking of friends. "Good morning, Flynn," she said as the big man moved into step beside her. "I'm surprised to see you up and about so early on a Saturday." Especially since he'd missed breakfast. Dammit, she'd actually looked for him this morning, as she'd served up pancakes and sausage.

"I slept in, but I hate to waste the whole day in bed. Not that there's anything *wrong* with spending the day in bed," he added suggestively.

The caution she had set aside for a while Thursday night was fully in place this morning. What did Flynn want? If he was just looking for a friend, he could turn to any man or woman on campus. Why her? She wasn't the prettiest, or the smartest, or the most influential woman on campus.

Did he think she'd be the easiest? Did he think that because her job was intellectually undemanding she'd be flattered that he was paying her this extra attention? So flattered that she'd fall on her back when he smiled at her and uttered a few kind words? If that was the case, he was in for a surprise.

Jack had taken advantage of her, making her believe that he cared about her. That he loved her. All along, he'd been using her, taking advantage of what she'd

thought had been love. Well, she wasn't eighteen anymore, and she hadn't been easy about anything for a
very long time.

"This is nice," Flynn said, glancing into the woods
on the right side of the track. Like her, he had dressed
in jeans and a T-shirt for the morning's exercise,
though his clothes fit in a different way than hers did.
His T-shirt was a little too tight. His jeans fit him almost *too* well.

Her jeans and T-shirt were both loose-fitting, easy
to move in and chosen for comfort, not to make an im-
pression on the opposite sex. So why was Flynn looking at her like he was impressed by what he saw?
Sometimes just the way he looked at her made her
anxious.

They left the wooded portion of the track behind and
moved into sunlight. From here, it was a few minutes
to the main building. She'd planned to walk the track a
couple more times, but suddenly the peace of the morning turned tense and uncomfortable.

"Enjoy it," she said, veering off the track and heading toward the parking lot. "It's going to be a pretty day."

There was a moment, she knew, when Flynn thought
about following her. But after a moment's consideration,
he continued walking briskly around the track and allowed her to make her escape.

Maybe she did like him, but there was no room in her
life for a man. All she cared about was getting her
daughter back, and nothing, not even Flynn Benning,
could distract her.

* * *

Laura Stokes had her hand up again. Great. "Yes?" Flynn said in a decidedly unfriendly tone of voice.

The girl's hand drifted down. "How long are we going to spend on the American Revolution? Usually we just spend a week on each chapter. We're getting behind. It's Monday, so we should begin a new chapter."

"We're going to study the American Revolution until you get it," Flynn said sharply.

"I *get* it," she said in soft exasperation. A couple of girls near her agreed.

"Not to my satisfaction, you don't." It didn't make any sense to him that the teacher who was currently sunbathing in Florida had skipped from chapter to chapter as it suited him, not studying American history in chronological order. Moron.

His other classes were more well behaved than this one. At least, they did their work quietly and didn't ask so many questions. He might growl at her, but he liked the fact that Laura Stokes had the guts to question him. The others didn't, for the most part, though he had caught one brave high school girl trying to nap through European History.

Flynn was about to assign another paper when the students were saved by the ringing of his cell phone. Sadie came up on the caller ID. He stepped into the hallway, ignoring the whispered voice that informed him cell phones were not allowed in class. Laura again, he knew it.

"Benning," he said as the door behind him closed.

"Is Cal with you?" Sadie asked.

"No. If you want Cal, call him. I'm not a freakin' messenger service."

"Someone got up on the wrong side of the bed this morning," Sadie said, a smile in her voice. "I asked about Cal because I don't want him to know we spoke. Not yet."

Flynn leaned against the wall beside his classroom door. "Kelly?"

"She was right here in Georgia, and I missed her by two days."

Flynn uttered a softly spoken single word that would have Laura reporting him to Dr. Barber, if she heard him.

"But this time, she told someone where she was headed. A woman she worked with. I explained things as best I could, and she gave me an address. Truman and I are headed that way."

"Where?"

"Colorado."

"Great," Flynn muttered. Every lead they found for Kelly Calhoun took them nowhere, and he didn't have great hopes for this tip.

"I just wanted to let you know where I'd be. Don't say anything to Cal until I come up with something solid."

"Got it."

"I'd drive straight through," Sadie said, exasperation in her voice, "but Truman won't allow it. He says I need my rest. For the baby," she added, a touch of wonder and joy in her voice.

Flynn's heart did a sick flip. "I can't believe you're

letting any man besides me tell you what to do, but in this case McCain is right. Get your rest. Cal wouldn't want you to make yourself sick."

"Don't mention sick to me," Sadie said with a groan. "I'd heard about morning sickness, but—"

"I gotta go," Flynn said abruptly, interrupting his one and only female agent. "I left a class of whiny little girls alone, and I hear 'em getting out of hand. Wanna trade jobs?"

Sadie laughed. "No thanks. Have fun."

Flynn ended the call and dropped his cell phone into his pocket. He opened the door on a classroom full of well-behaved students, who waited for him with an unnatural patience. A few of them whispered to friends, but they weren't anywhere near getting out of hand.

But that excuse was better than telling Sadie, or anyone else, that pregnant women were as tough for him to take as little girls.

Flynn Benning had obviously taken her abrupt flight from the walking trail as a rejection of some sort. He hadn't done more than nod and say hello for the past four days. In a way Tess was relieved. In another way, she kinda missed talking to him.

Maybe she should make more of an effort to get to know the other teachers. It was possible that Flynn was right, and what she really needed was a friend. After all, if Laura was here next year, odds were Tess would be here, too. Might as well make things as pleasant as possible.

Tess carried a plate of brownies and clean mugs into the middle school teachers' lounge. There was only one teacher present, Stephanie McCabe. That was a disappointment, since Tess was pretty sure she and the English teacher had nothing in common. Nothing at all.

But she might as well give it a shot.

"Hi," Tess said as she laid out the brownies and arranged the coffee mugs. She turned around and leaned against the counter. "I love your skirt. It's so…colorful."

Stephanie smiled widely. "Thanks. I made it myself."

"You did?" On purpose?

"I make a lot of my own clothes. It's so hard to find just what I want in just the right size." The English teacher wagged a finger. "You know, when you're off duty you should wear more color. I know Dr. Barber probably insists that you wear that godawful uniform when you're working, but even when you're not you wear such dull colors. Hot pink. You should definitely wear lots of hot pink."

"I like blues and greens," Tess said, wondering if this wasn't a really, really big mistake.

Stephanie pursed her lips in disapproval. "Turquoise, then."

"Next time I go shopping, I'll look for some."

The woman smiled, as if she'd accomplished something great in convincing Tess to try a new color. Then she leaned slightly forward and lowered her voice. "Have you heard about Serena Loomis and the new janitor?"

She hadn't heard anything, but she'd seen those two together enough to know that something was going on. "No, not really."

"It's shocking. Surely Dr. Barber has heard what's going on. I'm surprised she hasn't fired them both. If the students ever find out what they're up to, she will."

"They're adults," Tess said, trying not to sound too defensive. "As long as what they do after hours doesn't interfere with their jobs here…"

"I suppose," Stephanie said sharply, her smile gone.

Tess grabbed a couple of dirty mugs and headed for the door. Strike one. Not that she was surprised that she and Stephanie McCabe hadn't hit it off right away.

But the awkward conversation had only made her miss Flynn more—and she'd never expected that.

Flynn backed off for a few days, because he knew if he didn't Tess was likely to bolt. He'd scared her, somehow. So he smiled, and he complimented her on her cooking, but he didn't go out of his way to spend time with her. He didn't ask for seconds, and he didn't hang around the dining hall after everyone else had left.

But that didn't mean he wasn't keeping a close eye on her.

Lucky had her checked out, and from all appearances she was clean as a whistle. He'd lifted her prints last week, from a glass she'd left sitting on a dining hall table. They didn't match Austin's. He hadn't taken a hair to check for a match to the one blond hair that had been found, but she had the coloring of a natural redhead, and he'd checked very closely for pale roots.

Social Security number was legit. Her real name was Teresa, but Tess was a common enough nickname.

Stafford was her married name. A few years back she'd been married, for less than two years, to one Peter Stafford. *Irreconcilable differences* didn't tell him squat as to why the marriage hadn't worked. Didn't matter. It just so happened that she'd been on her honeymoon in Florida when Austin had committed the crime in Texas.

Tess was hiding something, but she was exactly who she said she was…and she definitely wasn't the killer he'd come here to catch.

They were making progress with the others, too, if you could call finding squat *progress*. Toller's prints weren't a match to Austin's, and neither were Loomis's. A dozen other teachers had also come out clean. They hadn't gotten McCabe's fingerprints—yet—and they hadn't been able to get their hands on one of her blond hairs, either, which were always sprayed into submission and didn't dare to fall out. The next step was to break into her room and have a go at her hairbrush.

Even though he no longer thought Tess might be Austin, something about the woman stunk to high heaven. Not literally. Literally she smelled amazingly sweet. Not perfumy, like some of the other teachers who apparently swam in cologne, but lightly fragrant, like woman combined with whatever she'd been baking that day.

Like he had time to notice how any woman smelled.

It was her college degree in computer science that stunk the most, figuratively speaking. Why was she working in the cafeteria, when she was as well educated as any employee in this school? Sure, the market for computer nerds had shrunk some in the past few years, but there was still plenty of work out there where she could use her skills, like teaching.

Flynn had survived more than a week of teaching history to girls who couldn't care less about what had happened last year, much less hundreds of years ago. Some were studious and did the work in order to earn a good grade, others did what they had to in order to get by. Still others all but dared him to fail them. They did half the work, they didn't study, their papers were sloppy and incomplete.

If he could've gotten away with it, he would have had half of them running laps after class, but he supposed that was Cal's job, for now. Maybe he could have them do push-ups when they misbehaved. Girls or not, they needed discipline. And as far as he was concerned, they still didn't get it where the American Revolution was concerned.

Since Tess had seemed more than happy to have him at a distance, he was surprised when, as she handed him a plate full of meatloaf and scalloped potatoes—it was Thursday evening, after all—she looked him in the eye and asked, "What are you doing after dinner?"

"Nothing," he said as he placed his plate on the tray that already sported a small bowl of salad. Next would be the apple pie, laid out at the end of the line for the diners to snag as they passed, just like last Thursday. Dr. Barber insisted on structure, even in the dining hall. "Why do you ask?"

She screwed up her nose a little, as if she wasn't sure

about what she was about to do. "Stick around?" she asked softly.

There wasn't time to ask why. A couple of giggling girls were coming up behind him. "Sure," Flynn said as he moved toward the pie. "Why not?"

Tess didn't want to do this, but who else could she turn to?

"Mind telling me what we're doing here?" Flynn asked as she led him up the narrow stairs. "I'd like to think you just couldn't stand it anymore and have been overcome with the need to jump my bones, but…"

She glanced over her shoulder and glared at him.

"But every now and then you look at me like that and I know I'm not going to be so lucky. So, what's going on?"

In the second-story hallway, there was plenty of space for him to walk beside her, and he did. Mary Jo was downstairs, finishing up the last of the dishes. The older woman mistakenly thought that Tess's meeting with Flynn was some sort of date, and since it pleased the older woman so much and was, after all, a plausible explanation, Tess had allowed Mary Jo to assume away.

"Mary Jo and I each have a room up here. The rooms aren't anything to brag about, but they're convenient and they come with the job." She pointed down one short hallway. "We're down this way, along with an old office where Dr. Barber sometimes comes when she wants to work uninterrupted. The other rooms up here," she continued down the hallway, rather than making her usual turn, "are used mostly for storage. Books, records, old furniture, that sort of thing. Dr. Barber is paranoid about school property being stolen, so the rooms are always locked. Always," she said again, with emphasis.

The hallway had a musty smell, as if the scent of old paper had seeped from the books and records and into the very walls.

"This morning, when I was headed down to start breakfast, I noticed that the door to the corner room was not only unlocked, it was slightly ajar."

"What time?" Flynn asked, all business now that he knew why she'd asked him to come upstairs.

"Five-fifteen. When I checked later, the door was closed and locked."

He nodded. "Did you ask Dr. Barber about the open room?"

"No. I went to see her after breakfast, but she'd gone to a one-day seminar in Atlanta. She won't be back until later. I didn't want to tell her secretary, especially after I found the door locked again. What could she do? Call the sheriff and tell him I saw a door ajar? They wouldn't take something like that seriously. They'd just laugh at me."

Outside the door that was once again locked, Flynn looked down at her. The lighting at this end of the hallway was dim, but she could see very well the stern cut of his jaw and the deadly serious gleam in his eyes. He believed her, thank goodness. She'd known he wouldn't laugh at her for being alarmed about something so apparently inconsequential.

"Why me?" he asked. "Why come to me with this?"

She pursed her lips, slightly. "Because you're one of those guys who fixes things when they're broken. A woman hands you a problem, and you solve it. It's part of your caveman mentality, your need to be leader of the pack, your macho and *occasionally* useful need to solve every mystery that crosses your path."

"Thank you, Red," Flynn said, adding after a moment, "I think." He tried the doorknob, and found it locked tight. "Hairpin?" he said, thrusting out his palm without turning to look at her. Of course, he knew she wore a few hairpins, when her hair was pinned up and back for work. At least she'd stuck the hairnet in her pocket as she'd led him up the stairs.

She gave him a hairpin. He bent it with capable fingers, then dropped down and gave his attention to the lock. In a matter of seconds Tess heard the tumbler turn. The door opened.

"Where did you learn to do that?"

"Misspent youth," he answered. "Surprised?"

"Not really."

They stepped into the room, which was exactly as it had been this morning. Cold, musty and apparently undisturbed. Tess reached for the light switch, but Flynn stopped her.

"No light. Someone might be watching."

She let her hand fall. "Right. I didn't think of that." And he had, of course. *Those guys* always thought of such possibilities.

"What's stored in here?" he asked as he walked to the corner of the room. Moonlight shone softly through the uncovered windows, keeping the room from being completely dark.

"Records, looks like," she glanced at a battered cardboard file box that caught a shaft of moonlight. "Old ones, it seems."

Flynn studied the boxes for a moment, puzzled and lost in thought. He looked at the old books stored on the bookshelves with just as much interest, and then he moved to the window. There were two windows in this corner room. Tess walked up behind Flynn to try to see whatever it was that he saw. There wasn't much. One window looked over the front entrance to the campus and the soccer field. The other faced the largest of two girls' dormitories.

Flynn let out a long, slow breath, and then he opened one window. Not only was it unlocked, the windowpane lifted easily and without making a sound. He closed and locked the window, then seemed to think again and unlocked it. The second window opened just as easily and silently. Flynn ran his fingers along the windowsill.

"It's been recently oiled," he said softly.

"Why?" Tess asked, her voice just as low.

"I can't think of any good reason," Flynn said, and then he muttered a vile word beneath his breath.

Movement caught Tess's eye, and she pointed to the figures that were running between this building and the dormitory. "Look. Someone's out there in the cold."

"I see them," Flynn said, unconcerned. "It's just the janitor and the math teacher, headed for the gardener's shed. Again."

"Oh," Tess said, deflated but more than a little relieved. Everyone knew about Dante Mangino and Serena Loomis. Everyone but Dr. Barber, that is, who would probably have a stroke if she thought anyone was having sex on the grounds of her school. The fact that the odd couple were so obviously enjoying themselves would be another strike against them.

Flynn left the windows, and everything else in the room, as he'd found them, and he locked the door as they stepped into the hallway. For a moment, he leaned against the wall and gave the matter some thought, and then he looked down at her. He had never seemed quite so tall and imposing as he did at this moment.

"Why did you come to me?"

"I told you, you're one of those guys who…"

"No, that's not what I mean. You didn't have to go to anyone with this. It's no big deal, right? Someone was snooping where they didn't belong. Anyone with a credit card or a hairpin could get into this room in a matter of seconds. Could've been some bored student poking around…"

"At 5:00 a.m.?" Tess asked sharply.

"There are a hundred logical reasons for this room being unlocked this morning. Why does it alarm you so much?"

She wasn't sure how to answer that. "Intuition," she said. "I don't know what Dr. Barber told you, but this month there have been a couple of break-ins. Nothing was taken, that I know of, but something just isn't right. If there's anything going on here that might in any way endanger—" she almost, *almost,* said *my daughter* "—the students," she continued after a very short pause, "then I want it taken care of." And Flynn Benning was the man to do it. How did she know that? Intuition, again, she supposed. "Do you really think it was just a bored student?"

"No. I wish I did."

They walked back down the hallway, moving slowly. Instead of proceeding down the stairs when they reached them, Flynn sat on the top step. After a moment's hesitation, Tess lowered herself to sit beside him. As usual, he looked slightly ill at ease in his khakis and button-up shirt, as if they were a costume he put on in order to do his job. She knew how he felt. There were times she felt like she was in costume, pretending to be someone she was not, in order to be here. His brow furrowed, a little, and his mouth thinned.

"What are you thinking?" she asked.

"You don't want to know."

"Maybe I do."

He relaxed there, sitting on the step, looking very much as if he belonged here, in spite of his outfit and the stern expression. Wide-shouldered and tougher than he had to be and cynical in a way that cut to the core…he was oddly fetching. The cut of his jaw and the width of his neck were masculine and handsome. Much as she wanted to think otherwise, she did not have time for fetching men who weren't going to stay. Even fetching men who *were* going to stay would distract her from her reason for being here.

Still, it couldn't hurt to look.

"I'm wondering if I can trust you as much as you apparently trust me," he finally answered, leaning back slightly against the top step. "I'm asking myself if I'm crazy for believing you. For all I know, you're yanking my chain."

"I'm not yanking *anything*," she said sharply, gathering her outrage and trying to stand. Flynn stopped her once again with that big hand on her wrist.

"I'm also wondering why I like you so much, even though you're obviously lying to me."

He pulled her in a little bit closer. Too close for comfort. "I'm not lying to you," she said softly. *Not about this.*

"Maybe not, but you're definitely hiding something. I can see it in the way you cut your eyes away when someone asks a question you don't want to answer, in the way your body language changes when someone gets too close. Getting involved with a woman who has secrets is a dangerous proposition, Red, even for me."

"I never asked you to get involved with me. In fact, I positively don't want you to even think about the word *involved* where I'm concerned. I just wanted you to look at the storeroom and see if anything was wrong." Something about the way Flynn held her wrist comforted her and made her panic at the same time. How was that possible?

"Don't you know that we caveman-type guys who like to fix things also have excellent instincts where women are concerned?"

She tried to gently tug her hand away from his, but

he wasn't letting her go. Not yet. "I never should've trusted you," she said. "I just should've waited for Dr. Barber to get back and…and… What are you doing?"

Somehow he had moved in closer, too close, and he had all but buried his nose against her neck. She could feel his breath, as well as the heat of his hand on her wrist. "You smell good," he said.

"I didn't give you permission to smell me," she said, not as harshly as she'd intended.

"You smell like cinnamon and sugar and soap."

Flynn didn't smell so bad himself, but she wasn't about to tell him so. His scent wasn't so easy to describe, but it was masculine and it teased her senses in a way she had not expected. For a moment she quit trying to pull away, and just sat there, too close and too involved.

"I don't have time for this," she whispered.

"Neither do I," he said, "and still I'm sitting here thinking…why not?"

Why not? There were a hundred answers to that question, all of them perfectly good. Tess had had her fill of demanding men, and to invite another into her life would be a disaster. She didn't have time for anything but her daughter, even though Laura had no idea who she was. Every spare moment was spent in watching and planning and dreaming. And waiting.

There was no time for the reality of Flynn Benning, sitting too close and smelling her. Smelling her, and holding her hand—sorta—and talking about secrets and getting involved and calling her Red. No one had ever called her Red before, and she liked it. Well, coming from him she liked it…and she couldn't afford to like anything about Flynn so well.

A heavy footfall on the bottom step jarred Tess to her senses. Flynn was jarred, too. They moved apart, but not soon enough to fool Mary Jo.

"I swear, the virus that sent the entire men's dormitory packing was the best thing to happen to this school in twenty years," Mary Jo said. "The math teacher's smiling all the time, Miss Stephanie has someone besides me to bug about skin care and it looks like the soccer team might actually be good enough to win a game this year. And to top it all off, here's Tess spoonin' in the stairwell. Looks like a major overhaul, to me, and about time."

Flynn released his hold on Tess's wrist, and she stood briskly to move out of Mary Jo's way. He stood, too, but he moved more slowly. "There's no spooning," Tess said. She tried to sound firm, which was difficult since her voice trembled.

Flynn headed down the stairs, moving at a leisurely pace. He moved like a man who was in complete control of every muscle in his fine body. He moved with a masculine grace, smooth and strong and powerful. She hadn't noticed that before. At least, she hadn't noticed so sharply that it took her breath away.

"Not yet," he muttered. And then he chuckled, before he turned the corner and stepped out of sight. "Major overhaul. Holy crap."

Chapter 4

Why that room? There wasn't anything valuable in that musty place, unless something had been well hidden in a box of files or under the floorboards. The oiled windows were disturbing. Was Austin looking for a way in? If that was the case, clearing the way into a first-story room window would've made more sense. Climbing to the second story or dropping down from the roof was likely to attract attention.

He didn't like where that left him.

"Possible sniper attack," Flynn said as he paced. "I can't be sure, and it goes against what we know of Austin, but from that vantage point he could target almost any place on campus. The parking lot, the main entrances to both dorms, the soccer field." That last possibility gave him a chill.

It was past ten, and the others were all present. Murphy, Cal, even Dante, who had managed to lose the overly ardent math teacher.

"Extra security on the main building?" Cal asked.

In the beginning, they had decided that installing any additional security might possibly spook Austin. When they'd thought they were looking for a thief who killed on the side, that made some sense. But what if they were looking for a killer who stole on the side?

"Cameras," he said as the thought occurred to him. "Murphy, I want you to discretely place cameras on both doors of the main building. It's got to be done at night, and in a way that won't tip off Austin, if he's watching. Anybody who goes in and out of that building will be recorded. Put something on the parking lot and near the dorms, but get the main building first."

Murphy nodded and made a couple of notes, planning for the long night ahead.

Flynn paced. "If we're looking for a hit man who stole those jewels and the painting in Austin to cover up the purpose of the murder, everything changes. He broke into the building in the past to scope out the best place to take a shot, and maybe to hide weapons and ammo. It's possible the weapon is or will be secreted in that room, so when the time comes all Austin has to do is get to the window and take his shot."

"Did you search the room thoroughly?" Murphy asked the question this time.

"No. There was no time, and I didn't want a light to alert Austin to the fact that someone was in the room.

I'll check it out again, during daylight hours. If nothing's there, I'll search again the next day."

"If he's watching, Austin might notice you visiting the main building more often than you should," Cal noted.

"I'll take care of that," Flynn said.

One week from Saturday was the start of parents' weekend at the Frances Teague Academy. If murder was the purpose of Austin's presence here, that was the most likely time for attack. In their investigations they had found nothing that might denote a member of the faculty as a target, and that left the parents. Or the kids. Surely even Austin wouldn't sink so low. Besides, Austin had had access to this campus and the people here for months, and the security had been lax, until recently. If a student or a teacher had been the target, they'd already be dead.

Unfortunately, there was more than one political figure among the parents who would be there next weekend, and almost all of them were rich enough to have the kind of power that could make them the target of a paid assassin. There was no way to tell who that might be, and if they canceled the planned event Austin would just find another time and another way. The objective of this job would end up just as dead—and Austin would be twice as careful in getting it done.

He also had to consider the possibility that Austin wasn't working alone. His accomplice could be almost anyone. A teacher, an administrator, that weird counselor who didn't spend a whole helluva lot of time with the kids. It didn't even have to be someone new. With enough money, Austin might've bought himself an accomplice. Anyone here could be involved.

Flynn looked to Dante. "Ever see Loomis go into the main building when she shouldn't?"

"No," Mangino answered. "Meals only."

"You don't by any chance know where she was at five-fifteen this morning."

"No."

"Too bad." He looked at Murphy. "McCabe?"

Sean shrugged his shoulders. "I don't know where she was at 5:00 a.m., but I'd say she was sleeping. She doesn't strike me as being at all dangerous. She's just interested in selling me more crap for my face. Apparently I have committed a sin by never wearing the proper SPF sunblock."

In truth, they had no proof that Austin was here on campus. He could be hiding and waiting in town. With his recon done, he might not show himself until the last possible minute.

He hadn't expected it, but a wave of something powerful washed over Flynn. No matter what happened, Austin couldn't be allowed to put the students here in danger—even if it meant warning him off, even if it meant letting him go. Somewhere along the line these students had become his girls…and that was a real disaster.

"From here on out, we're armed at all times," Flynn said. "Keep it discreet, but if Austin shows himself we will be ready."

* * *

Bright and early Friday morning, Flynn presented himself at Dr. Barber's office. She bristled at him, the way she often did. The old broad was accustomed to intimidating all her employees, and she obviously recognized that Flynn didn't intimidate easily.

He closed the door behind him, and crossed his arms to glare at the woman who sat at her desk like a stern matriarch.

"Ms. Stafford discovered a storeroom door open yesterday morning."

The woman paled. "I knew I should have found a way out of that blasted seminar. As unlikely as it seemed, I wanted to believe your presence here would turn out to be unnecessary. Apparently this isn't over."

"Not by a long shot."

"If the disturbances are continuing, then you and your men have not been very effective, Mr. Benning. What are we going to do about that?"

Flynn placed his palms on the desk and leaned forward slightly. The old bat was accustomed to being in charge of every detail. So was he. Their meetings were never pretty.

Barber was not intimidated by his glare, even though she was old enough to be his grandmother and probably weighed ninety-eight pounds. Would she get hysterical if he told her it was possible Austin was a hit man, not a thief? Possible, but unlikely. The woman was tough as old, rusty nails. If she hadn't been the one to report the initial break-ins and insist that something be done, he might wonder if she was aligned with Austin, in some way. Assassination for money could be big business, and with enough money you could buy anyone.

Well, almost anyone. Not everyone was for sale.

Until he knew more, there was no way he could tell Dr. Barber or anyone on her staff what he suspected. No matter how they tried to keep the information contained, word would get out and someone would panic. What little control he had over the situation would disappear.

He left Dr. Barber to her mound of paperwork, headed for the kitchen and then made the turn to take him to the stairway. All was quiet. Breakfast was over, class would begin in twenty minutes. The second-story hallway was deserted, and he slipped the lock on the storeroom with an old credit card. Once inside, he closed the door and leaned against it.

If he was right, a weapon was hidden here—or soon would be. He started in the far corner, looking in file boxes while making sure they did not appear to have been disturbed when he moved on to the next box. Papers, papers and more papers were all he found. There wasn't time to look at everything this morning, but he'd be back. He'd go through every box in this storeroom.

A sniper would want to prepare his nest. He'd want to sit by the window and look out over the grounds, he'd want to get comfortable here. He'd want to go through the motions, a few times.

He, or she? Anything was possible.

Lunch on Saturday was always simple. Sandwiches and soup, usually, with cookies or brownies for dessert.

It had been a quick lunch and a quicker cleanup, which left Tess free to enjoy the afternoon. It was one of those great February days warmed by a promise of March. Spring wasn't here, but it was coming. You could smell it on the air and feel it in the sunshine.

She sat on a bench near the soccer field, which was deserted at the present time, though she thought maybe the older girls would be practicing here this afternoon. The last couple of practices she'd watched had shown the teams were much improved. Calhoun was doing a good job. The kids were going to miss him, when the old coach returned.

Must've been one heck of a virus, to keep those affected out for nearly two weeks. Whatever the illness was, it hadn't spread beyond the men's dormitory, thank goodness. She could only imagine what a nightmare it would be if something like that ran rampant through the campus and the town. The unnamed virus had laid four men low for much longer than it should've, and their replacements had been making themselves right at home. She wished the stricken men would all get well soon, so that Flynn Benning would be sent home, once and for all.

Even though she didn't see him often, she thought about him more than she should, and spotted him at a distance, and replayed every conversation they'd ever had again and again in her head, wondering if she should've said or done something different. Wherever he came from, there were probably a dozen girlfriends who fawned over him and vied for his manly attentions. There just weren't that many men out there who looked like Flynn. He was a dangerous man—dangerous to her, at least.

"Hi, Red."

Speak of the devil… "Mr. Benning."

He sat beside her and draped one long, muscular arm across the back of the bench. Since it was Saturday, he had left his khakis and button-up shirts behind. Black jeans and a dark gray T-shirt suited him much better. Had his legs always been so long?

"I tell you that you smell good, and the next thing I know you're calling me Mr. Benning again."

Tess moved slightly away from him. She could not afford to notice how long his legs were, or admire the strength in his arms, or realize how blue his eyes were when he wore such colorless clothes. "You did a little more than tell me I smell good."

"Did I?" he asked as if he truly didn't remember.

"Go away, Flynn," she said, closing her eyes and trying her best to blot him out of her sight and her memory.

"Can't do that," he said casually, as his arm dropped down to her shoulder. "I need you to take me up to your room."

That got her eyes open, quickly. "What?"

"You heard me. Okay, we don't have to actually go to your room. I want another look at that storeroom you found disturbed, and I can't just waltz on in without arousing suspicion."

"I overreacted," she said, shifting away from his possessive arm. "It was probably someone looking for an old file, and they forgot to lock up, and then they went back and locked the door—"

"And oiled the windowsill," Flynn added.

She turned her head to look at him. He was deadly serious. Worse, he was worried. "What's going on?" she asked softly.

"I can't tell you."

"Then I can't help you."

His eyes narrowed. She imagined he'd intimidated a lot of people, men and women, with that glare. Not her. She'd seen worse.

"Damn, you're stubborn," he finally said. "I'll make you a deal. You walk in with me, I'll have a look around and if I find anything I'll let you in on my suspicions."

"You don't need me for that."

"People might be watching," he said in a lowered voice.

"No one here cares if you—"

"Maybe not," he interrupted, "but that's a chance I can't take."

She was about to argue, when a familiar voice stopped her. She looked past Flynn, and for a moment she couldn't believe what she was seeing.

Laura and Bev wore big smiles…and so much makeup she almost didn't recognize them. "Oh, my God," Tess said in a hushed voice. "You look like…you look like…"

"Hookers," Flynn finished for her. "Little, red-lipped, sparkly hookers."

Laura was in the lead, as always, and her smile died. "Mr. Benning, you obviously don't know anything about fashion."

"Yeah, but I do know a thing or two about…"

Tess elbowed him before he could finish, and he dutifully shushed.

"Is Stephanie McCabe selling makeup to the students?" Tess asked as she stood and cautiously took a couple of steps toward the girls.

"They're free samples," Bev said shyly. "Don't you like it? She said we looked smashing."

"Smashing what?" Flynn muttered.

Tess turned and looked down at him. "Would you hush? You're not helping matters at all."

Laura pointed with an insolent thirteen-year-old finger. "Is he like your boyfriend or something? I thought you didn't like him."

"You said you didn't like me?"

Tess turned to look down at Flynn again, and he sighed. "I know. Shutting up, now."

"This is just so wrong," she said as she raked a thumb over the makeup that was caked over Laura's cheek. "You're beautiful girls, both of you, and this is…it's…" Words failed her.

"Mr. Benning has been talking about freedom this week," Laura said indignantly. "Not just big freedom, like of a country, but of personal freedom, which is what it's all about, anyway. We can protest in the open and hold meetings and put our opinions in the newspapers, even if they're not popular opinions. Isn't it my personal freedom to wear makeup if I want to?"

"I don't think that's what our founding fathers had in mind," Tess said as she rubbed at another thick spot of foundation on Laura's cheek.

"We were thinking about going to town this afternoon," Bev said in her usual gentle way. "The boys usually don't look at us at all, but if we look more sophisticated they'll look, won't they? I really would like to have a boyfriend, one day."

"Bev!" Laura whined, spinning on her friend. "You can't tell *them* we're going to town."

The younger students leaving campus on their own was a no-no, but the older girls had been known to walk to town to shop or get fast food or see a movie. Still, Laura and Bev were just thirteen, and they had no business walking to town alone. Tess got a chill just thinking about her daughter confronting the big bad world unprotected. Of course it would happen, eventually, but now? So soon?

"I know I'm not supposed to speak, but we're getting into my territory, since I am, after all, the gender they're trying to impress." Flynn stood and crossed his arms over his chest, a gesture which made him look bigger and more intimidating. Studying the girls, with a peculiar expression on his face, he shook his head slowly. "I suppose it's not terrible, if you don't mind looking like a hooker, but…"

Tess elbowed him again. "That's not helpful."

"You look like you're trying to imitate a pop star or an actress," he said, his careful eyes on Laura's face, and then Bev's. "Maybe this kind of look is fine for them and the world they live in, but it's not real. It's not right. There's nothing prettier than clean, unadorned skin on a woman's face. Look at Tess, here."

"Don't look at…"

Before she could say more, Flynn reached out and

touched her cheek. "Her face is clean and smooth and perfect, and if it was covered in goop I couldn't do this." He raked his finger along her cheek, and the girls' eyes went wide. She didn't want it to happen, but her stomach did something funny, and her knees went a little weak. Just from that one, wandering finger on her face. She wanted to give Flynn a stern glance and tell him to stop, but she didn't dare look at him. Her mouth went dry, her fingers trembled. Finally, he dropped that finger that was driving her up the wall.

"You," Flynn said to Laura, bending down slightly and giving her the glare. "You have fabulous green eyes, and right now they're lost in a sea of bubblegum pink cheeks and scary red lips. Without the makeup you have a nice little smattering of freckles across your nose...."

"I hate my freckles," Laura said. "Ms. McCabe showed me how to cover them up."

"Ms. McCabe is likely jealous because she doesn't have any. The freckles are cute. Show them off, kiddo." He turned his study to Bev. "And you're no better than your friend here. Your skin is beautiful, and it's hidden under that goop. The color on your face takes away from your eyes, too. They look more blue without that unnatural crap. Both of you have great smiles. Do you know what happens if you wear all that gunk on your mouth and you smile? Lipstick on the teeth, which let me tell you is not attractive. Boys *hate* that."

"Do you really think we look better without makeup?" Laura asked suspiciously.

"Absolutely," Flynn answered. "Now, please, go

wash off that crap. And the next time Ms. McCabe tries to give you anything to cover up those pretty faces, you tell her that the only skin care product you need is soap. That really pisses her off."

Bev's thin shoulders wiggled, a little. "You really shouldn't say things like crap and piss and hooker to us, I don't think."

"Yeah," Laura said. "But we won't tell." She actually smiled. "I mean, we're not in class or anything, and we are old enough to engage in an adult conversation outside of class."

"Damn skippy," Flynn said.

"Does that mean yes?" Bev asked.

"It means absolutely, positively yes," Flynn clarified. "Now, go wash up. Use *soap*. Get all the crap off and this afternoon I'll drive you into town for a little while." He raised a censuring finger. "No makeup, and no boys. You're too young. But we can grab some ice cream or something."

Laura's eyes went wide. "Really?"

"Yeah. As long as Ms. Stafford here agrees to ride along with us."

Flynn looked at her, awaiting an answer. The girls stared at her, too, and she could swear they were holding their breath. "Sure. Sounds like fun."

"Cool," Bev whispered.

"*Very* cool," Laura agreed in a louder voice.

Tess watched the girls walk away. There was an extra bounce in their step as they left. Of course there was. A handsome, if somewhat older, man had told them they were pretty. He'd noticed their eyes and their smiles and Laura's freckles. He'd offered to drive them to town for ice cream. She could love him right now, just for that.

"Wow," she said. "Not bad. Do you have kids?"

"No." His voice was a touch too crisp, not at all like the charming tone he had used with the girls. He started walking toward the main building, his stride so long and fast that she couldn't quite catch up with him. Since she owed him one, she followed anyway.

The main building was quiet on Saturday afternoon. Dr. Barber was not in her office; her secretary, who lived in town, had the day off; the useless counselor never came in on the weekend; and the dining hall and kitchen were quiet. Flynn and Tess didn't see anyone as they walked inside and climbed the stairs.

Flynn kept his back to Tess, until he had a chance to gather his composure and face her without emotion. He'd been fine, just fine, until she'd asked him if he had kids.

While he'd been talking to Laura and Bev, he hadn't even thought of his own daughter. And then Tess had asked the question and unexpected emotion had hit him like a ton of bricks.

He didn't ask her for a hairpin today—she wasn't wearing any. Instead he took a credit card from his wallet and slipped the lock. It was even faster than picking the lock with a bent hairpin.

"Nice," she said softly. "Another product of your misspent youth?"

"Yeah," he said as he walked into the storeroom. Tess

followed him in and closed the door behind her, but she stayed there, leaning against the closed door and watching him.

It didn't look as if anything had changed, but that didn't mean Austin hadn't been here. He began in the far corner and worked his way back, as he had yesterday morning, searching behind and inside boxes, keeping his eyes on the task at hand and trying to forget the regret that had come up out of nowhere and hit him surprisingly hard. It had happened long ago, it didn't matter anymore, he was being a freakin' woman…

"Are you going to tell me?" Tess asked after he'd been searching the room for a good ten minutes.

"I told you, if I find anything…"

"That's not what I'm talking about, and you know it."

Might as well not play games. She was too smart for that, she saw too much. "No use in it," he said without looking at her. "The past is past."

"I know," she said, her voice not much more than a whisper. "But every now and then the past rises up and bites you on the ass."

Flynn's head snapped up at her observation. No, she wasn't smiling; it hadn't been a joke at all. Tess didn't joke around, much, that he'd seen. She was always serious, always watchful. She surprised him. What on earth was she doing here?

He liked her this way, dressed in jeans and a pretty sweater, her hair loose and falling over her shoulders. When he'd touched her cheek he'd been surprised, by her reaction and by his own. She was a real woman, in a sea of deception that ranged from the superficial—too much makeup and a put-on attitude—to something so deep and dark most people in the world never touched it. How was it possible to hide the ability to do murder behind a false front? He didn't know how that was done, but he knew it happened.

He finished a quick search of the room and found nothing…again…and then he sat down beneath the window and stretched out his legs.

"I was married, once," he said.

"Divorced?" she asked as she walked across the room to join him.

"I wish," Flynn answered. "My wife was killed in a car accident. She was eight months pregnant at the time. A little girl. Neither of them made it."

"Oh, Flynn." Tess sat beside him and laid a comforting hand on his arm. "I'm so sorry."

Flynn bristled at her words and her touch. He wasn't asking for sympathy, not from her or anyone. "Don't be. It was fourteen years ago, a long time. It was hard for a while, but I have a good life, now. I like my work and I manage to be happy enough most of the time, but now and then…" Now and then the past did rise up to bite him on the ass. "Elizabeth never got to be thirteen. I didn't get to warn her away from leeches like McCabe, or drive her to town for ice cream, or watch her tackle that awkward phase between being a little girl and becoming a woman." There was more, so much more, but he didn't dare say it aloud. Elizabeth had never been five and swung on a playground swing, or eight and played soccer, or…or…or…

Tess unexpectedly leaned in and rested her head against his bicep. She was warm and soft, and genuine, and her touch affected him in a way he had not expected. He didn't do close, not where women were concerned, and here she was. Close, in more than a physical way.

"I'm sorry," she said softly. "Working here must be difficult for you."

If he was smart he'd set her aside and stand up and change the subject. He didn't talk about Denise and Elizabeth, not ever. It was his own secret pain, locked away in a place where it didn't have the power to hurt him anymore. But he didn't push Tess away, and he didn't change the subject.

"Not always, just…sometimes."

"You didn't ever think about getting married again, having other kids?"

Flynn's heart danced as if it had been given a nice little jolt. His personal nightmares were never about monsters or pain or the unknown. They were about funerals; they were about searching an empty house, room by room. "No way. I'm not going to take the chance that I'd have to go through that again."

For a moment, he thought Tess was going to say something. Maybe she'd try to make him feel better, or tell him that things would be different if he took a chance again, or just tell him again that she was sorry. But ultimately she said nothing, which suited Flynn just fine.

He didn't want sympathy or platitudes, but having her so close was nice. She was warm and soft, and she smelled good. Today she smelled like vanilla.

"We don't have to take Laura and Bev to town today," she finally said.

"Yeah, we do." He wasn't about to break a promise to two kids just because he'd been slammed by an unexpected bout of grief.

"I can take them myself, and we'll come up with an excuse for you to stay here, if it's too hard."

"No. I'll be fine." The grief faded, as it always did, and Flynn actually found himself smiling. "They really did look like hookers," he said. "Even with the conservative clothes they were wearing, and those goofy smiles…I swear, I'm going to have to have a talk with Ms. McCabe."

Tess patted his arm. "Maybe you'd better let me handle that."

"I can handle it," he argued in a gruff voice. "I'm not going to get girlie again and weep all over the English teacher."

Tess lifted her head and looked up at him, and she wore her own soft smile. "Actually, I wasn't worried about *you*."

He raked one finger against the underside of her chin. There was something about this woman that got under his skin, and if he was smart he'd run like hell. He couldn't afford to let anyone or anything get under his skin.

Kissing Tess was the worst possible thing he could do, given the situation, but he did it anyway. He did it because she smelled like vanilla, and because she didn't sit here and baby him after his minor meltdown, and because he could. She was surprised, at first, but she didn't pull away and after a moment she kissed him back.

It was the kind of kiss a man could get lost in, the kind of kiss that could wipe away the past. Her lips were so soft and sweet and giving, and she tasted so good he didn't want ever to take his mouth from hers. The way her lips moved and tasted…she wasn't any more anxious to end this than he was.

Flynn didn't do sex for the sake of sex, not anymore. One-night stands were empty and meaningless, and while he had once embraced both those qualities, he'd outgrown the concept years ago. He wasn't looking for a relationship that would last more than a few days or weeks, either, which left him in between. It would take an extraordinary woman to make him change his ways.

Tess Stafford was an extraordinary woman.

Her mouth moved over his, gently and with more than a little trepidation. She held her breath, she trembled. It had been a while since she'd kissed a man, he could tell that by the way she seemed surprised by the sensations the kiss elicited. A small, soft moan broke from deep in her throat.

She had nice curves. A part of him wanted to explore all those curves here and now, but he didn't. He did place one hand on her hip, though, and he allowed it to rest there almost possessively while the other moved over hers.

Tess wasn't a one-night-stand woman, any more than he was a one-night-stand man.

Flynn was the one who ended the kiss, which left both of them unexpectedly dazed.

"I like vanilla," Tess said when she found her voice.

Flynn smiled. "So do I." He bent his head and took

a long, deep breath while his nose was buried against her neck. And then he quickly kissed her neck, and again she quivered. "You smell like vanilla."

"I meant ice cream," she said quickly, and with a touch of panic in her voice. "Vanilla ice cream. We need to go collect the girls. I have to be back here in two hours to fix supper."

Flynn brushed a strand of auburn hair away from Tess's face. She didn't know who he was or why he was here, she continued to keep secrets from him and everyone else and when this was all over he couldn't stay.

Kissing Tess had been a mistake, but he wasn't sorry it had happened.

"You never did tell me what's going on here," she said as she moved slightly away from him. "Are you going to?"

"Not now," he said as he stood. "It'll take more time than we have. Tonight, after dinner?"

Tess sighed as she stood and brushed off the dust she'd picked up while sitting on the floor. "Tonight is fine," she said. "But you'll have to talk while you help me do dishes. Mary Jo is staying in town tonight, and she'll want to get home before it gets too late."

"I can do dishes." He followed her from the room. "I'm actually very good at doing dishes."

"Brag too much and you'll have yourself a new part-time job," she teased.

When they reached the stairway, Flynn turned back. "Did I lock the door?"

"Yeah, I'm sure you did," Tess answered.

"Let me double check." He knew damn well the door was locked, but he wanted to make sure that if anyone else went into that room he'd know about it. He attached the almost-invisible thread at the top of the door. As long as it was intact, he'd know the door had not been opened.

And even though Tess turned him on, he wasn't yet ready to share all his secrets with her.

Chapter 5

Thorndale, Georgia, was a fairly small town, just big enough to have an ice-cream parlor, a two-screen movie theater and a nicely manicured downtown park. There was small shopping center at the edge of town, but the shops that lined the streets of downtown were also adequately stocked and well kept, and it was a much more fun place to spend a Saturday afternoon. The buildings here were old, a few of them dating to the early twentieth century, but most had been renovated in the past ten years.

The economy was fueled primarily by the Frances Teague Academy and a small industrial complex near the mall. As far as Tess was concerned, it made for a community that was just the right size. Not too small; not too big.

She didn't come into Thorndale often. She lived at the school, afraid that if she left even for a few hours she'd miss something. Laura might need her and she wouldn't be there. That wasn't a logical fear and she knew it, but recognizing the logic didn't make her any less fearful of failing and losing her child again.

Thanks to Flynn, she was taking her daughter out for ice cream. As far as she was concerned, it was just another reason to forgive him for being one of those guys.

She should hold the kiss against him, but she didn't. It had been nice. More than nice—the intensity of the feelings she'd experienced had surprised her, in a good way. It had been a long time since she'd allowed herself to feel passion of any kind for anyone or anything but her daughter. Flynn Benning definitely made her feel passionate. He made her feel like a woman who'd been hiding for too long, who'd been afraid for too long. He made her feel…different, and alive, and hopeful.

Good thing he was a substitute who didn't plan to stay long.

They'd traveled to town in Flynn's vehicle. She'd expected him to own a pickup truck with oversized tires, as men of his type usually did, but instead he drove a rather unremarkable gray sedan. The car didn't look like much, but she suspected from the sound of the engine that it had a few more horses under the hood than it should've, which did not surprise her at all.

They parked a few blocks away from the ice-cream parlor and walked slowly down the sidewalk, window shopping and listening to the girls talk, enjoying the day.

She'd never seen Laura or Bev so animated. Their good mood was Flynn's doing, she knew. He'd made them feel special, at least for today. He'd made Tess feel special, too, in an entirely different way.

Flynn had been right in his observation about the girls being caught between little girl and woman. They were so vulnerable, and they had so much to learn—so much of life stretched before them. Tess wanted to protect Laura from those who would try to take advantage of this fragile time in her life, who would twist her emotions and her uncertainties to their own advantage.

She wanted to protect Laura from men like her father, and she didn't know that she'd ever get that chance.

Tess did her best to put all her uncertainties about the future out of her mind, for a while. Laura and Bev looked like little girls again, with their faces scrubbed clean and their hair pulled back—thanks to Flynn. On the outside he was tall and well muscled, physically capable to the point of breathtaking. But on the inside, his heart was just as strong. It took a strong heart to do what he'd done today, to put aside his own pain and take care of these little girls who were not his own.

She and Flynn had responded to their losses in very different ways. He refused to take the chance of losing someone he loved again, no matter what the cost. In a way she could understand that; what he'd been through must've been very painful, and locking his heart away might have seemed like a good idea, at the time. But the cost was high. In order not to lose, you had to give up so much. Love, family, someone to talk to in the dark at the end of a long day. She had put those things aside, for now, but she hadn't given up on one day having it all.

When she'd thought her child was lost to her forever, she'd been desperate to replace the baby. It was the reason her marriage hadn't worked. She'd wanted a family more than anything in the world, but Peter kept saying he wanted to wait a few years before they had children. It hadn't taken him long to figure out that she had never loved him the way a wife should. She'd loved the idea of him as the father of her child; she'd loved the picture in her mind of the family she wanted and needed to create.

Tess still wanted more children. She was thirty-one, and that certainly wasn't too old to have another baby or two. Maybe she didn't have a lot of time, but she wasn't over the hill, either. Once she had the situation with Laura settled, one way or another, then she'd think about that family she'd always wanted. With any luck, she'd actually have the chance to do something about it.

She wanted to give Laura brothers and sisters. Whether or not Laura was even aware of those siblings would be another matter...one Tess had not yet decided.

"Vanilla for me," Flynn said as they came to a stop outside the ice-cream parlor. The small shop was surprisingly busy, considering that it was February and the temperature was anything but balmy.

"Vanilla," Laura said with a widening smile.

"Make it three," Tess said.

Bev raised her hand shyly. "Chocolate chocolate chunk."

"There's a rebel among us," Flynn said as he opened the door and allowed the women to precede him.

Just inside the door, Tess looked back and smiled up at Flynn. If this outing was difficult for him, he didn't show it. Whatever emotion he'd experienced in the storeroom, it was behind him, now. He'd put it out of his mind, or at least appeared to have done so. She had a feeling he was one of those men who didn't give away much of themselves, so in truth she didn't know if this was painful for him or not. He wouldn't tell her, and she'd never be close enough to him to see for herself. Too bad.

A familiar couple walking down the street caught her eye. The janitor and the math teacher passed by, holding hands and talking, finishing one another's sentences and laughing. She didn't know Dante Mangino well enough to know about him, but Serena Loomis had never looked so happy. No, not happy. Content. Apparently the mismatched pair had more in common than sex, after all.

Major overhaul, indeed.

A large dishwasher took care of most of the dishes, but they all had to be rinsed, and there were a few that needed to be scrubbed. Oddly enough, Flynn didn't mind helping out. It was a fitting end to a decent enough day—meltdown aside.

Students and teachers who lived on campus had been in and out of the dining hall for most of the evening, but at last all was quiet. Flynn had locked the main door of the building behind Murphy, who had been the last to leave…with a plate of leftover brownies to see him through the night.

After Flynn had returned to the kitchen there had been other chores to see to. Sweeping, washing down the counter, putting dishes and silverware away. For a few quiet minutes he'd thought—and hoped—that Tess had forgotten why he was here tonight. And then she asked bluntly, "So, what are you looking for in that storeroom?"

He considered the question for a minute. How could he respond? He wanted to be honest with Tess, since he had a feeling they were going to end up in bed together sooner or later. But how honest could he be? Other than his own team, he trusted her more than he trusted anyone else around here—which wasn't saying a whole helluva lot.

When he listened to his gut, he knew Tess was all right. Not only had she told him about finding the storeroom open, she obviously cared about the students.

He had never been very good at playing games, not with the people he cared about. "We have reason to believe that a man certain factions of the government would like to get their hands on is hiding here on campus. Or nearby," he added.

Tess set aside the towel she'd been using to wipe down the counter. "You work for the *government?*"

"Well, not exactly. I was hired by a consultant that on occasion does some work for the…"

"You're a *spy?*"

"No, I'm not a spy. Exactly. I'm more like a private investigator."

She walked toward him, not at all intimidated. "I knew it. You, and Coach Calhoun, and the janitor. Murphy, too? I knew something about the four of you wasn't right."

"Tess, I can't…" He didn't get far in telling her what he couldn't say.

"Is this man you're looking for big trouble or little trouble?"

He didn't answer right away.

"I'm not asking for details, Flynn. I just want to know if the man you're looking for is dangerous."

Flynn hesitated a moment before answering, "Yes, he is."

Tess's angry green eyes said it all. "You're here looking for a dangerous man and you don't even bother to tell the other teachers so they can protect the students." Her face actually blanched and she stopped short of coming close enough to touch.

"For all we know he could be working with one of the teachers," Flynn explained. "Or she. We don't know for certain if the person we're looking for is male or female."

A barely audible gasp warned him she didn't like what she was hearing. "Mangino is sleeping with Serena Loomis in order to *spy* on her?"

"Of course not."

Tess's face went absolutely white. There was more than anger in her eyes, now. Flynn saw hurt and confusion and betrayal. "That's why you were so nice to me, isn't it? You're a spy and a sneak. Am I still a suspect, Mr. Benning?"

"If you were, would I be telling you this?"

"I don't know," she said softly. "I have no idea how your mind works."

"Very logically, normally, but since I came here…not so much," he admitted.

Tess looked him in the eye. She would make a terrible poker player. Every emotion she experienced showed on her face, and Flynn wished he hadn't told her the truth. He should have found a nice, safe lie. She looked betrayed and confused, as if he had failed her by not being the man he had pretended to be.

"I wouldn't be telling you this if I didn't trust you completely. Someone here could be working with the person we're looking for." His patience was wearing thin. "Someone here could *be* the person we're looking for. Don't look at me like I just told you I had a third nipple and a pointed tail."

Tess didn't take the bait and get angry, storming out and saving him from saying anything more. "Has anything you've told me about yourself been true?" she asked.

"Some."

She laughed, without humor. "Can I pick 'em or what?" One step took Tess back and away from him.

"I'm telling you the truth now."

"Why?"

Because I like you. "Because I need your help." Dammit, he was going to have to scare her a little bit more, or else he was going to lose her completely. "We came here looking for a thief who killed a man who surprised him midjob a few years back. At least, that what's we believed until you took me into that storeroom. I think it's possible that the man we're looking for went into that storeroom to study the view. He oiled the windows so he can open and close them without making any noise. I believe it's possible that he plans to shoot someone from one of those windows. Next weekend, most likely, while all the parents are here."

He actually saw her tremble at the news. "You can't let that happen."

"I don't plan to."

"The girls will be out there with the parents. What if one of them gets in his way? What if…" Her expressive face showed the horror of the *what-ifs* that were running through her mind.

"I plan to catch him before he has the chance to hurt anyone."

This time she walked toward him, and she poked him in the chest with one very insistent finger. "You better stop him, because if you don't, when next Saturday gets here I'll put an end to the situation myself. I'll tell everyone who will listen that their lives are in danger, and I'll herd every child on this campus to a safe place. I won't let any killer, male or female, get near any one of these girls, do you hear me? If you want to catch him, you do it someplace else. You use someone else for bait besides my…my girls."

Flynn finally lost his temper. "I'm not using anyone for bait, dammit. Do you think I'd actually line up a bunch of kids on the lawn and wait to see who gets shot at? Do you think I'm that kind of man?"

Tess hesitated, but not for long, before answering, "Yes, I do."

Every man she'd ever fallen for had disappointed her, in one way or another. Jack, Peter…they were all the same, beneath the skin. Flynn Benning was no different. At least she hadn't fallen too far, this time.

He followed her up the stairs. "I'm sorry to drag you into this," he said in a lowered voice. "But what choice do I have? I need to be able to come in and out of this building as I please, without arousing suspicion. If you and I are involved…"

She made a loud grunting sound that told him of her disgust. "Won't work. Dr. Barber will fire me if she thinks I'm sleeping with one of the teachers, and I can't afford to lose this job."

"Dr. Barber knows why I'm here. I'll explain that this is a ruse, that you're helping with the investigation, and your job won't be in jeopardy."

Tess felt selfish for worrying only about Laura, but dammit—she was a mother. She had every right to worry about the safety of her only child to the exclusion of all else. "I'll help under one condition."

"Name it."

In the hallway, she stopped. She wanted to be looking Flynn in the eye when he said yes. Or no. Maybe she knew him well enough to see that he was telling the truth, or not. Maybe he would have second thoughts about lying to her again, while his eyes were locked to hers.

She looked up into a handsome face that just hours ago had had her thinking about things best left unexplored. At least she'd found out he was playing with her before it went too far. Another broken heart would do her in.

"If you don't catch the man you're looking for this week, you cancel parents' day. You put a guard around the girls, or else you move them off campus to a place where they'll be safe until you find the man you're looking for."

"Canceling the plans will spook him."

"I don't care."

Flynn raked his thumb across her cheek. "Okay," he said in a lowered but seemingly honest voice.

"Nobody gets hurt," she whispered.

"Damn skippy."

He leaned down and kissed her again, and even though she had the chance to back away, she didn't. She liked the way Flynn kissed her; she liked the way her body responded to his—completely and instantly and intensely. Her knees wobbled, her insides quaked. It was a strictly physical response, without any danger to her heart.

But even in her heart, she wanted to believe him, she wanted to trust that he was telling her the truth—this time. In the heat of anger she'd accused him of putting the students in danger, but surely the man who had made Laura and Bev smile, who had set aside his own heartache to take them out for ice cream, who had so convincingly told them how pretty they were wouldn't put their lives in danger.

Tess let Flynn kiss her, and she even kissed him back. She had forgotten how powerful a kiss could be, how it could change the air and the sensations of the entire body and the workings of the mind. She rested her hand against his arm, so solid and strong, so masculine. She drifted into him, more and more. Her body shifted closer and tighter, and there was a moment when she felt as if she could never be close enough. Her body and her mind wanted more of this—more kissing, more Flynn. And it wasn't going to happen.

The moment ended, and she stepped away from the man who'd kissed her so well. "I wish I didn't know who you really were," she said. If she still thought Flynn was a substitute teacher, here for perfectly ordinary and legitimate reasons, they'd still be kissing. She might even ask him to come to her room, where they might or might not end up doing more than kissing. Her heart knew she'd been betrayed again—her body hadn't yet accepted that fact.

"You asked for the truth and I gave it to you," he said as she continued to back away. "I'm one of the good guys, Tess."

"Maybe so, but I still don't trust you."

"I'm sorry to hear that."

She wanted to ask Flynn what—among all the lies he'd told her—was truth. Had he really lost a wife and child, or had that been a lie intended to illicit sympathy and that first kiss? Had he ever taught at a military school? Was his name really Flynn Benning?

It didn't matter, now.

"I'm going to bed," she said. "Don't forget to lock the building when you let yourself out." After all, there was a killer on the loose, very possibly on campus at this very moment. Tess shuddered. She hated the idea of sleeping alone in this big, empty building tonight.

But it was preferable to the alternative: Asking Flynn, or whatever the hell his name was, to sleep with her. Alone was better. She'd been doing *alone* for a long time, and, dammit, she was getting very good at it.

Change of any kind was disturbing, especially when it came so close to the climax of a well-planned job that had taken months of precious time.

Flynn Benning walked out of the main building, angry and frustrated. From the shadows, Dale Emerson watched and smiled. Benning had been chasing Tess Stafford with the usual vigor of a man of his type, and apparently tonight had not gone as he'd planned. It was almost comforting to know that *everyone's* plans could be shot to hell.

The virus that had emptied the men's dormitory had been alarming; the men who had moved in as substitute teachers and personnel had proved to be just as alarming, in their own way. They were too astute, too curious…and too much of the same type for Dale's comfort. It was no accident that they were here, at this place at this time.

But it didn't matter who they were, if they were legitimate or not. They knew nothing of importance, and by the time they got their act together the assignment would be over.

Dale was very selective in choosing jobs. Killing people paid well, and with the little caution and lot of skill it required, paid assassin had turned out to be the perfect profession. No two assassinations were the same. Some had been made to look like accidents, others like suicides, still others like robbery gone wrong. Others still were simple executions, accomplished by gun, or knife, or in one case, a silk stocking. This one had been more difficult than the others, since the target moved so frequently and erratically.

But a week from now, the job would be done and Dale would be on the way to Cancún for a well-deserved vacation. Who knows? Maybe the recent invasion of the campus by these irritating men who did not belong could be used to an advantage.

Sadie sat in the passenger seat and watched the door to the apartment. Maybe the address had been bogus, and she and Truman had wasted their time coming all the way to Colorado. People liked Kelly. They lied for her; they protected her. It was part of the reason she'd been so hard to find.

They'd been watching the apartment for two days. No Kelly. No nothing. Sadie's heart broke, for Cal. And for Kelly, too, who didn't know that her brother was alive and looking for her, or that the stepfather she'd thought she'd killed had died of a heart attack days after her escape.

Not that it would have mattered. No jury in the world would have convicted Kelly of murder. The bastard had raped her once and was trying to do it again, when she'd fought back. A heart attack was a much too easy way for a man like that to go. At least Kelly had gotten in one good lick before she'd escaped.

All the information Kelly had gotten back then, about Cal dying in Camaria and about her stepfather passing away shortly after she'd hit him over the head with an iron skillet and run for her life, had been wrong. And at seventeen, she hadn't thought to question anything. She'd be twenty-five, now, just barely. It was time for her to stop running.

Cal wanted his sister to come home, and Sadie wanted to be the one to make that happen.

Truman reached across and took her hand in his, as if he knew she'd started to worry. "We'll find her."

Sadie took her eyes from the apartment door. "What if we don't?" Her husband wasn't crazy about her staying so involved in this investigation, now that she was carrying a child. Once the baby was born, and Truman ran for sheriff and they settled into a routine—would she be able to set this obsession aside? "I promised Cal I'd find her."

His fingers threaded through hers. "Not giving up, are you?"

"I don't want to."

He lifted her hand and kissed it. "The girl I married never gives up. I know that without a doubt."

"I love you, you know." She leaned across the seat to kiss him.

"Yeah, me too."

The kiss was much too short. A flash of light caught Sadie's attention, and her head snapped around. She'd missed seeing anyone enter, but a light in the apartment they'd been watching was on.

Chapter 6

It was almost two in the morning, but Flynn wasn't asleep when his cell phone rang. He was stretched out on a too-short couch, fully dressed, his mind spinning.

He flipped the phone open and answered with, "Benning."

Murphy responded simply. "Someone's trying to break into the main building."

Flynn didn't wait for more information. He ended the call as he moved up and off the couch, grabbed his gun and ran. One thought took precedence over all others: Tess was in that building, alone.

He ran at the head of the pack, but he was not alone. Murphy was right behind him, and so was Cal. After a moment, Dante joined them, which meant it could very well be Serena Loomis breaking into the building. At this point, only a handful of those on campus were not under some sort of suspicion.

Fingerprints had cleared some of the employees, but that didn't mean they couldn't be working *with* Austin.

They moved as quietly as possible, keeping to shadows and making little noise. They barely disturbed the quiet of this night.

Flynn kept thinking about what Tess had said to him earlier tonight, about getting the girls out of here even if it meant losing the quarry. Was he willing to risk anything and anyone to get Austin? Was he willing to risk her life as well as his own? It had been a very long time since he'd felt as if he were obligated to protect anyone who hadn't paid him for the honor. He was a bodyguard, an investigator, a soldier, a hired gun unlike Austin in that the jobs he took were just. He took his calling seriously, but he did not get personally involved. Not until now.

The would-be burglar Murphy had seen trying to pick the lock on the main entrance, by way of the hidden camera that was mounted over the main door, had moved on to a window and was trying to force the lock. Five foot six or seven, Flynn guessed as he ran toward the suspect. Black hooded sweatshirt, with the hood up and covering the face. Black pants, black boots. Small. Too small.

By the time the intruder heard Flynn approaching, it was too late. Escape was attempted, with a burst of unexpected speed. Since the culprit's hands were empty,

Flynn stuck his weapon into his waistband at the spine, increased his speed and tackled the black-clad burglar. They both went tumbling to the ground. Woman, he decided immediately as he crushed the small body to the ground.

"Ouch," a whiny voice rose up from beneath the hood, and Flynn raised up just enough for the perp to lift her head slightly and push back the hood, exposing a brunette ponytail.

Not a woman, exactly. A girl. Melody Matthews. Seventeen years old, antisocial, smart-mouthed, and enrolled in Flynn's European History class. He'd caught her sleeping in class, once.

"What the hell are you doing here?" he asked. He no longer pinned her to the ground with his body weight, but he had her trapped, with one hand manacling her wrist.

The others had surrounded them, and they were all as surprised as Flynn had been.

"Get off of me before I report you to Dr. Barber, you pervert."

Flynn released her and rolled away. "Yeah, well, you can report yourself for trying to break into her office at the same time, kiddo. I'll ask one more time, what are you doing here?"

She sat on the ground, obviously still shaken. Flynn sat nearby. She wasn't going anywhere. Even if she jumped up and found a burst of speed, one of the guys would catch her. Besides, where was she going to go?

"What is this, some kind of new school security?" she asked. "Can't a girl go for a walk around here without getting thrown to the ground by a grown man twice her size?"

Flynn jerked his thumb to the window. "Not in there, you can't. Don't make me ask you again."

Well and truly caught, what choice did she have? Melody Matthews was a senior, and according to her file she'd been sent here after being kicked out of a number of other high schools, public and private. Her father had brought her here as a last resort. No mother mentioned, that Flynn could remember, just the father. Maybe that's why the kid was so messed up. She didn't socialize much, that he'd been able to see. In fact, she seemed to openly ignore the other girls, though he had seen her talking to Laura and Bev on a couple of occasions. Maybe she felt as if all three of them were outcasts, of a sort.

Flynn hadn't seen any serious trouble from Melody, but she definitely had an attitude. Right now, the attitude wasn't doing her any good. Long brown hair escaped from her hood and fell over her shoulder and her cheek, and she took deep, uneven breaths. Her knees were actually shaking.

"They keep copies of the tests in Dr. Barber's office," Melody finally said. "You can't get near them during the week, with her and her secretary and the school counselor always nosing around, but I thought on the weekend…"

"You came here to swipe a test?" Flynn interrupted.

"Yes," Melody said without apology. "There's big money in that kind of information. *Hello*."

The insolent hello got Flynn's hackles up even more than they already were. He glanced up to Cal, before finally rising to his feet. "Is the sheriff on his way?"

Cal nodded. "Yes, he is."

"Wait just a minute." Melody stood and brushed a bit of dirt off her black jeans. "You called the sheriff? I didn't *do* anything. You can't charge me with anything but being out after curfew, you numbnuts."

"That's not a very nice way to talk to the people who hold your future in the palms of their hands," Murphy said without rancor.

"Okay, this little incident doesn't have to go on my permanent record, does it?" Melody asked, her tone changing quickly. "I mean, I learned my lesson, really I did."

Flynn leaned in close and lowered his voice, "Go back to your room and go to sleep and forget any of this happened, and maybe if you're lucky we'll forget, too."

"Thanks. You're the best, really." With that she ran toward the girls' dormitory. Flynn turned to watch her go, and Tess stepped into his line of vision.

Her hair was down, and she wore a thick but short robe over silky pajamas. There was some kind of small print on the pj's, but in this light he couldn't tell what it was. Fuzzy slippers kept her feet warm, and her hair was tousled, as if she'd come here straight from bed. She looked more beautiful than any woman he'd ever seen.

"What's going on?" she asked as the other guys moved away.

Flynn waited until they were out of earshot before he

answered. "False alarm." Almost without pausing, he added, "Dammit, Tess, I don't like the idea of you staying here by yourself."

Her head cocked to one side, and she rubbed her hands along her arms as if to chase off the night's chill.

"Neither do I," she finally said.

Tess had heard the noise long before she'd realized that it was Flynn outside the building. Her heart had almost come through her chest as she'd quickly assessed the possibilities, but as soon as she knew Flynn was there, everything had become instantly better. Not fixed, not perfect. But definitely better.

Leading him into her apartment was a bit uncomfortable, but also felt right. She wasn't prepared for company, but her place was clean enough. Her quarters here were really quite nice, better than she'd expected when Dr. Barber had mentioned an apartment above the kitchen. It consisted of a large living room with a very small kitchenette, which was equipped with a coffeepot and a small refrigerator. The attached bedroom was small but had a nice big closet and a decent-size bathroom with a claw-foot tub and a more recently installed showerhead.

Flynn had left his room without even a jacket on this cool night. Something had sent him running. With a gun.

"How did you know the girl was here?" she asked as he closed the door behind him and surveyed her living room.

Flynn sighed before answering, and she knew she

wasn't going to like what was coming. "There's a newly installed camera over the front entrance, and one at the back."

"I don't suppose I should be surprised," she said coolly. "What about this room? Cameras? Maybe a bug or two?"

"No."

"Why should I believe you?"

He didn't answer; there was nothing he could say.

"Is your name really Flynn Benning?"

"Yes. Everything I told you, except the part about…"

"It doesn't matter," she interrupted crisply. "I just wanted to know if I'd been calling you by your real name or an alias. Not that it's all that important. I was just curious."

For a long moment, Flynn just looked at her. No smile, no scowl, no nothing. Then he said, "I'll stay in the hallway."

Tess turned to the kitchenette. "No, you won't. I'm going to make us some coffee. Decaf. Somehow I don't think I'll be drifting right back to sleep." The sounds of someone rattling around beneath her window had made her heart jump, and it was still pounding too hard and fast.

"Maybe you can find a movie or something on television," he said, obviously not anxious to sit up with her. Sounded as if he preferred the hallway to her couch.

"Maybe your room comes with cable, but mine doesn't. The few stations I get show infomercials late at night, and that's it." She continued making decaf as if Flynn would stay with her for a while, when she was far from sure that he would. She listened as the coffee began to brew. The door didn't open and close, so maybe he wasn't going to run. Yet.

She turned and leaned against the counter while she studied him. She wanted to believe that he was, as he'd said, one of the good guys. But dammit, she was so tired of lies.

"I can get you off campus," he said. "We'll come up with a believable cover story and—"

"No," she said sharply. "I'm not running."

"There's no reason for you to stay here," he said, sounding very logical and authoritative. "It doesn't make any sense."

"The man you're looking for won't be alarmed when yet another employee flees from the school?"

"I don't care if he's alarmed or not," Flynn said, just short of losing his cool. "I want you out of here."

She walked toward him, on fuzzy-slippered feet. "Why?"

He didn't answer.

"What difference does it make?" she asked again.

"Don't make me say it, Red."

"Don't make you say what?" she asked, exasperated and no longer afraid to let it show. "That you like me? That you're starting to feel responsible for me? That you care whether or not I get hurt?"

"There's no freakin' reason for you to stay!" he shouted.

There was a very good reason, not that she could afford to tell him or anyone else about Laura. "If you

want to do some good around here, convince Mary Jo
to stay in town with her son for the week, not just on
the weekend. Her arthritis makes it difficult for her to
move quickly, and if anything happens, getting her out
of the building or out of the way will slow me down."

His jaw was sharp, his chin stubborn. "I think I can
handle that. Maybe you could move to town, too."

"Then where's your excuse for spending the night
here?"

"I'll think of something," he said, growing agi-
tated again.

"I'm not running."

"Dammit, Tess…"

She took a step closer. "I'm not running."

"You don't have a lick of common sense."

"Apparently not, since you're here instead of sleeping in the hallway. Which leads me to something else
you can do for me." She was close enough to touch him
now, but she didn't. "People will see you coming and
going, I know that, and they'll assume whatever they
want to assume. But be discreet where the kids are concerned. I don't want them to think I'm the kind of
woman who'll open up her bedroom for any man who
comes along, a man who will be gone next week."

"They won't think…"

"Just do it."

"I will, but…" He reached out and touched her face,
in that way he had. Like it or not, she loved the way he
touched her. It made her feel connected, in a way she
had forgotten. "The girls here love you. I see it. I saw it

from the first day. There's nothing you or I can do to make them love you any less."

"If that's true, then it's all the more reason to be careful about the example I set for them. Young impressionable girls don't need to see a woman they respect getting involved intimately with a man who obviously doesn't care for her in anything more than a casual way."

"And you won't move to town, not even for a week," he said, not bothering to argue that he did care for her in more than a casual way.

"No."

He shook his head, took a deep breath to calm himself and flicked one long finger against the pajama collar that peeked out from her robe. "Pink bunnies," he said, studying the small print.

She was more than a little embarrassed, and sounded defensive when she said, "These pajamas were on sale, and they're very comfortable." And no one was ever supposed to actually *see* them, unless Mary Jo stopped by to borrow coffee or sugar.

"They're…cute," Flynn said, and then he leaned down to kiss her. For a moment Tess thought he was going to try to change her mind that way, with a brush of his lips and a flicker of his tongue. But the kiss was brief, and when it was done he went to the kitchenette counter, grabbed a coffee cup from the cupboard, and filled it with fresh decaf. He didn't actually talk to her, but she did hear him mutter "stubborn woman," once.

Flynn took the sagging chair that had come with the

apartment, leaving the couch for Tess to have to herself, after she'd poured her own coffee.

"For the record," he said when she was settled, "what I told you about losing my wife and daughter was the truth, and that's not something I tell just anybody."

Her heart skipped a beat. "I'm sorry."

"I'm not finished," he said sharply. "Don't interrupt."

She raised her eyebrows, then took a long sip of hot decaf.

"I don't do casual," he continued. "I'm forty years old, for God's sake, and landing in bed with a woman I hardly know just to get my tractor cranked is too freakin' pathetic."

Tess took another long sip of coffee. There were plenty of responses to that statement, but Flynn had more to say and she certainly didn't want to interrupt him.

"If you stay here, you're going to distract me at a time when I don't need distractions. I'd like you to reconsider moving to town for the week, or else coming down with some illness that'll get you away from the school for a few days."

"Another bout of your fictional virus is likely to raise a red flag," Tess said.

He didn't say it out loud, but she read the answer on his face. He didn't care.

"I'm not going anywhere," she said. "Deal with it. If I distract you, that's your problem." She took another long sip of coffee.

"Pigheaded female," he muttered.

Oddly enough, the decaf and butting heads with

Flynn eased Tess back toward sleep. Her heart began to pound at a somewhat normal rhythm, and her eyelids were getting heavy. Flynn looked very much like he was headed in that direction, too. Angry or not, he was tired.

She tossed him a pillow and blanket before she closed her bedroom door, and after a few minutes more she heard the front door to her apartment open and close.

Flynn Benning was sleeping in the hallway.

It was easy enough to get Mary Jo out of her apartment. Her son and his wife "won" a trip to Florida, a prize that required their immediate departure. Grandma would be staying with the kids for the entire week. Her three grandsons were all in public school, but afternoons—and nights—Grandma Mary Jo would be there to feed them and keep them out of trouble.

That meant Tess had the kitchen to herself, after three in the afternoon, so Flynn volunteered to pitch in and help.

Annoying physical attraction aside, there was no reason for him to let this one stubborn woman get to him. Maybe he should forget about his no-casual-sex rule and go to town just to get laid. There was a seedy bar just past the city limits, and that would be the place to go. Maybe then he wouldn't itch every time he looked at Tess Stafford.

But one-night stands were still pathetic, in his estimation, so he suffered and itched without going to town. He also grumbled. A lot.

By Monday night Flynn had moved into Tess's apartment, more or less, and started sleeping on the couch.

The ancient sofa was too short for him, and it was lumpy, but it was preferable to the floor. He supposed he could move into Mary Jo's room, but he wanted to be as close as possible—just in case something happened.

He was very discreet, as Tess had asked him to be, when coming here at night and when leaving in the morning. She was right about that, though he hadn't actually told her so. Impressionable girls didn't need to see the adults in their circle behaving like they had no control.

Even Dante and Loomis were fairly careful. The teachers all knew they were involved, but the kids were oblivious—unless they noted that their usually irritable math teacher was smiling a lot more lately, or that the hallway floor directly outside her classroom seemed to be more well-mopped than the rest of the school.

No one had entered the storeroom since Flynn had placed that piece of string over the door frame, but time was running out. In three days, on Saturday morning, the campus would be teeming with parents. Targets, if his new supposition about Austin was right.

Every morning, he woke to the smell of Tess's coffee, and this morning was no different. It was almost worth sleeping on this damn sofa, to wake this way. Slowly, with the scent of that coffee in his nose and the sound of Tess's feet shuffling in the kitchen, while she tried to be quiet. She was an early riser. Usually he was awake by 5:15, so that he could get out of the building before the kids were up and about, and Tess was always up before him.

"Do you ever sleep late?" he asked as he rolled into a sitting position. His voice was gruff, his neck stiff.

"Not since I started working here," Tess said as she poured him a cup of coffee and crossed the room to deliver it to him.

After he drank half of that first cup, he went to the small bathroom he and Tess had been sharing for the past few days. It wasn't fancy, but he'd seen worse, and it was twice the size of the little bathroom in his room. While he was in there he splashed water on his face, trying to scare some alertness into his fuzzy brain.

"We need a vacation," Flynn said as he walked into the main room and reclaimed his coffee. Instead of returning to the couch, he sat in the chair that wasn't much more comfortable. "Someplace warm, where there are no kids and no bad guys, and we don't have to get up at the crack of dark, and there are large, soft beds all around." He tried to work the crick out of his neck with a twist, but it didn't work.

Tess stood behind him. "No kids and no bad guys," she said as she laid her hands on his neck and began to rub. "I don't know. I could definitely do without the bad guys, but I kinda like the kids."

Flynn closed his eyes and let her massage his neck. "They do tend to grow on you, don't they?"

"Yeah."

The way she was with the girls…the sadness he sometimes saw in her eyes…the fact that she was here when she should be someplace else…they all hinted at secrets she had not yet shared. "So, what about you?" he asked. "Do you have any kids?"

He expected a quick "no," though he wasn't sure

whether or not that answer would be the truth. If Tess
had kids, she'd have them with her if she could. Maybe
he hadn't known her very long, but he did know her.

She kept rubbing his neck, and she didn't say no.
After a minute or so she began to speak softly. "When
I was eighteen, I had a baby. A little girl. I really thought
the father loved me, like I loved him. Finding out I was
pregnant was scary, but I truly believed that he would
marry me and take care of us. Forever and ever," she
added wistfully. "But of course that's not the way it
happened. His family had money, and a girl like me...I
wasn't good enough for him, or for the rest of the family. His mother actually accused me of trying to trap
Jack by getting pregnant."

Flynn muttered a single word meant to convey his
opinion of this mother.

"My mother was already gone," Tess continued, "and
my dad was sick. So when they said they'd arranged a
private adoption with the family lawyer, I didn't fight.
Not much, anyway. How was I going to take care of a
baby on my own? I didn't have a job, my father was in
and out of the hospital...and I was so scared."

Flynn laid his hand over Tess's, and she stopped mas-
saging. Her hands and her voice trembled.

"So I signed away all my rights and gave my daughter up for adoption, in exchange for enough money to
take care of my dad's medical bills and see my way
through college. Not a bad deal, huh?"

Flynn tugged on Tess's hand and gently drew her
around so he could see her face. There were tears in her

eyes and she'd lost the color from her lips. He pulled her onto his lap, where he held her hand and raked one thumb across her jawline.

"If I could take it back, I would," she whispered. "But there are some things you can't take back, not ever."

"Baby, that sucks," he said. "I'm sorry."

"Yeah," she whispered. "I don't know why I told you. I never tell anyone. When anyone asks if I have kids, I always just answer no. It's the truth. I don't *have* her."

He knew why she'd told him. She knew he cared about her. She knew there was nothing casual about this relationship, whether he was sleeping on the couch or not. He gave her a quick kiss, one meant to offer comfort and sympathy and kinship. "Have you ever tried to find her?"

"The adoption was private, and the lawyer who handled it is retired."

"So? There have to be records, somewhere. My agency has found lots of kids over the years. Kidnapped, runaways…"

"No," Tess said sharply. "I'm not asking you to fix my mistakes, that's not why I told you."

"But…"

"Sometimes it eats at me, and there's not anyone in my life that I can share this heartache with. I don't want you to rush out of here and try to make things right for me. Some things can't be made right, Flynn."

"But that's what I do, Red. I make things right."

"Not this time. This time I just want you to listen and understand, and maybe hold me a little while."

That he could do. He pulled her to him and she laid her head against his shoulder.

The door to the apartment opened, and a woman walked into the morning light. Finally! Sadie squinted. The hair color was different—blonder—and the uniform was different, but it was Kelly Calhoun—the girl Sadie had once known as Kathy Carson.

Sadie reached across the seat and shook Truman awake. "That's her," she whispered.

Kelly walked down the stairs to the parking lot. Instead of heading for a car, she started walking down a long, narrow sidewalk. Headed for work, most likely, to pour coffee and work for tips until someone asked a question that made her uncomfortable and she moved on.

Sadie eased out of the car. Truman did the same, on the driver's side. Together they followed Kelly at a distance, closing in slowly. They couldn't afford to lose her, not now when they were so close.

When they were several feet away, Kelly sensed their presence and looked back. Her eyes widened, and she stopped. "Sadie?" she asked suspiciously. "What are you doing here?"

"Looking for you," Sadie said.

It was the wrong response. Kelly took off running, and Sadie followed. Truman cursed, ordering Sadie to stop.

"Cal sent us!" Sadie shouted. Kelly didn't even slow down. She left the sidewalk, cutting through the lawn, and down a gently sloping hill. Shoot, Cal was short for Calhoun, which was probably not what Kelly had called her brother, as a child. "Quinn!" Sadie yelled. She was a fast runner, but Kelly was just as fast. Truman's bad knee slowed him down, but he kept up better than he should've, considering the rocks they encountered. Just ahead there was a thick stand of trees. If Kelly ran in there, if she knew her way around…she'd be lost again.

"Quinn is alive and looking for you!"

Kelly stopped, turned and raised her hand to keep Sadie at a distance. She was already breathing hard, just as Sadie was. Sadie obeyed the signal, and Truman pulled up behind her.

"She's pregnant," he said to the woman they'd been chasing. "Don't make her run."

"I'm fine," Sadie said. She smiled gently at Kelly. "When I married him I didn't know he was such a worrywart."

"You guys are…" Kelly waggled a finger from Sadie to Truman and back again, and in answer Sadie flashed her wedding ring. "Congratulations." Kelly took a single step back, and out of breath or not she was very much ready and able to run. "I like you Sadie, I do, but someone is pulling your leg. My brother Quinn died years ago, in…"

"Camaria," Sadie said. "Only he didn't die. Long story, but in a nutshell the people there didn't plan for him to ever make it home. He did, though. He's been looking for you for years."

Kelly shook her head. "Even if that's true, I can't go back. I killed…"

"You didn't kill anybody," Sadie explained. "Your

stepfather died days after you ran away from home. Heart attack. It's a good thing, too, because if he'd been alive when Cal got home, your brother would be in jail for murdering the SOB."

Kelly took a single step toward Sadie. A small step. "I want to believe you, but I still think someone's messing with your head, and mine."

Sadie lifted her hands, palms up. "Cal…Quinn, I mean. Dark brown hair, green eyes like yours, mean as a snake if you cross him but the best man around to have watch your back when trouble comes." Truman laid a hand on her shoulder. "Except you, of course, honey," she added. "Your stepfather used to hit him. He has a scar." Sadie pointed to her temple. "His first scar. Beer bottle. He would never tell me about it, but his wife thought that detail might come in handy if I found you."

Kelly's eyes sparkled with tears. "Quinn's married?"

"Yeah. Livvie's very sweet. She's a schoolteacher, and she's absolutely crazy about Cal."

Kelly took two tentative steps toward Sadie. "I want to believe you."

"Then believe." She couldn't help it that her own tears stung her eyes. Damn hormones! No matter how tender the moment, she was usually not a teary person. "Please, please let me take you back with me. I've found plenty of lost kids and taken them home, but I want to see you and Cal reunited more than anything else."

"Why?" Kelly whispered.

"Because he's family."

Kelly finally moved close enough for a hug, and

Sadie held on tight. She held on as if Kelly would disappear if she let go. "You were so hard to find!" Sadie said as she hugged Cal's sister tight. "How did you do it? We're good at finding people, but you were a definite challenge."

"I never stayed in any one place too long," Kelly said, "and every now and then someone would look at me funny or ask an odd question or just be too interested. When that happened, I moved on pretty quick. There was always another small restaurant who'd let me work for tips, or a motel that needed rooms cleaned."

"You have good instincts," Sadie said. She let go of Kelly, reluctantly, and reached for her cell phone.

Kelly laid a trembling hand over hers. "Not over the phone. If Quinn really is alive, I want to see him face-to-face. I won't believe this is real until I actually *see* him."

Sadie nodded. It wasn't too much to ask. Besides, she really would love to see Cal's face when he was reunited with his sister.

Sadie was bracketed by Truman and Kelly, and she held on to their hands as they walked up the hill. Truman for comfort; Kelly because she still wasn't sure the girl wouldn't try to bolt again. She could leave Benning's with a clear conscience, now, this last job completed successfully.

The major would likely need a new female agent, sooner or later.

"You gave us quite a run, girl," she said as they approached the apartment steps. She was anxious to get out of here and head home, but Kelly needed to pack her things. She'd likely left without them more times than she could count, so maybe she didn't have much to pack. Still…this time they weren't going to run.

"Sorry," Kelly said softly.

Sadie laughed. "Don't apologize. I was just wondering if you were interested in a new line of work."

Chapter 7

Maybe she shouldn't have said so much this morning, but when Flynn had asked if she had any kids the words had come spilling out, much too easily. She'd told him things she'd never told anyone else. And like it or not, it had felt good to share her biggest mistake with someone.

No, not just with *someone*—with Flynn. She wouldn't have said so much to anyone else.

There were just a few teachers in the lounge this afternoon, as Tess arrived with a plate of brownies. Flynn was not one of them; he had World History this period, if she remembered correctly. Leon Toller was sitting at the table in the corner, his head bent over a large, slick art book. Stephanie McCabe was checking her makeup and Serena Loomis stared out the window, looking as if she'd lost her best friend.

Tess would have been happy to drop off the brownies and leave without engaging any of the teachers in conversation, but Serena Loomis homed in on her before she had a chance to depart.

"Brownies. Great. Just what I need, something else to go straight to my hips."

Tess's initial reaction was to snap back, *You don't have to eat them,* but she kept the comment to herself. Besides, the woman barely had any hips at all. She could use a few brownies.

"They're just too good to resist," Serena said in a less-caustic voice, as she grabbed one square. A small one. "I can't cook at all. Mr. Benning must be in hog heaven. I imagine he thinks he's found the ideal woman."

Tess's eyes went wide. Yes, she and Flynn did spend time together, but he'd been careful not to reveal too much...especially the past few days.

"Don't look so surprised," Serena said. "The man is helping you in the kitchen, for goodness' sake. He's washing dishes and wiping down tables. A man like Flynn Benning doesn't do things like that unless he's in love."

"You've made some wrong assumptions," Tess said softly. *Very* wrong.

"Okay, he's in lust," Serena said. "Call it whatever you want, the man is obviously obsessed with you."

Tess turned toward the door. "I have to go."

Serena fell in behind her. "I have to see Dr. Barber this afternoon. Mind if I walk with you?"

Tess's heart sank, but she answered, "Sure."

March was coming, and Tess could almost smell it in the air. Spring. Life. That new green that was so fresh and fragrant. February was hanging on, but March was right around the corner. Tess normally loved March. She loved leaving winter behind for the gentleness of spring.

Serena waited until they were well away from the building before she spoke again, and she kept her voice low…as if she expected someone to be listening. "Be careful, Tess."

Again, Tess was startled by the teacher's words. "What do you mean?"

The usually caustic woman's voice was almost wistful as she answered. "You think you can have a fling and it won't mean anything. Sex is fun, right? And when a delicious man comes along and he thinks sex is fun, too, well…why not? The opportunity to have frantic, meaningless sex with a gorgeous man doesn't come along every day. Especially not around here."

"I'm not…" Tess began.

"And then one day you look at this gorgeous man and realize that it isn't meaningless anymore. You like him. Maybe you even love him a little, and trust me, you can't fall in love with a man who's seven years younger, and has long hair and *tattoos,* for God's sake, and works as a janitor. You can't get serious about a man who thinks limericks are literature and that matching tattoos are a sign of commitment. Do you know what my father would say if I went home and introduced…" Suddenly

Serena went quiet, and she picked at an invisible wrinkle on her spotless tailored white blouse.

"We're not talking about Flynn anymore, are we?" Tess asked.

Serena sighed. "Get a clue, Tess. We haven't been talking about Flynn since we left the teacher's lounge."

"About that matching tattoo thing…" Tess began.

Serena ignored her. "Help me out here. You're a rational, down-to-earth, intelligent woman who just happens to make the best brownies I've ever tasted. Tell me what to do. Tell me how to make what's happening to me revert back to meaningless, wild sex again. I'm a logical woman myself, and I like things to add up just so. Two plus two is always four, and numbers don't lie. My personal life has never been so cut and dried, but I've always been analytical. I don't get carried away. I don't…" Again, Serena sighed. In the afternoon sunlight, with spring on her face and maybe even in her heart, the math teacher was prettier than usual. There was a flush to her cheeks, and a sparkle in her eyes— even though at the moment there was also a touch of panic in those eyes.

"Matters of the heart aren't logical," Tess said, and she immediately thought of Flynn and her confession, and the fact that she liked him so much when she shouldn't like him at all.

"This fling with Dante isn't so much fun anymore," Serena said. "I mean, it *is,* but…I'm scared about things I haven't even thought about for a very long time. Does he love me? Will my father like him? How many kids

will we have? Will he be here next week? I feel like I'm
fifteen again, and it's not any more pleasant now than
it was then." She sighed. "I love him, and I know he's
going to hurt me, somehow. They always do, you know."

"Yeah, I know."

As they reached the main building, Serena opened
the door for Tess. "You're not going to be any help at
all, are you?"

"Sorry. I don't know what to tell you."

"Well, my original warning still stands. Be careful."

"I always am."

But lately, had she been careful enough?

Something was wrong with Dante, no one had been
in the storeroom since that first day, which made Flynn
think his suppositions about Austin's plan might've been
wrong, and he thought about Tess far too often during
the day. In other words, his normally well-ordered world
was screwy as hell.

Even when he was caught in the middle of a difficult job, certain things were a given. His team was re-
liable, his hunches were right-on, and he didn't indulge
in distractions.

Screwy.

He was down to two and a half days before parents'
day got underway, and he was beginning to agree with
Tess about one thing; he couldn't allow any of the girls
to get caught in the crossfire. Moving them quickly and
quietly would be a problem, especially since only those
teachers who had been cleared of suspicion could be al-

lowed to know that the kids were being moved. Most of the teachers had been cleared, thanks to fingerprint analysis and hair samples, but that wasn't enough anymore. If Austin was working with someone, as Flynn suspected, then they had to start all over. Anyone was fair game.

He'd ordered Lucky to look into everyone's past again, organizing a new team and interviewing neighbors, coworkers at past jobs, old lovers. For now, no one was entirely free of suspicion.

If they could manage it, when the time came, they'd move kids only. He wouldn't take the chance of putting a killer on the bus with those girls.

It was possible Austin had been spooked, and the plan had been neutralized. While it meant missing the bastard, this time, Flynn didn't mind that possible scenario so much.

He'd fiddled with the rabbit ears on the small television in Tess's apartment, and he'd added some aluminum foil. The picture was crap, but he'd found a basketball game that gave him an excuse for staring at the screen. He'd already checked the perimeter of the building once, and an oddly moody Dante and a grumpy Cal—who was missing his wife—would patrol during the night. Maybe Austin would see what was going on and know that his plot had been discovered, and he'd be scared off.

Just as well. Another time and another place would suit Flynn just fine. A school was not the place for this showdown.

He was surprised when Tess sat next to him on the

Get FREE BOOKS and a FREE GIFT when you play the...

LAS VEGAS
GAME

Just scratch off the gold box with a coin. Then check below to see the gifts you get!

YES! I have scratched off the gold box. Please send me my **2 FREE BOOKS** and **gift for which I qualify**. I understand that I am under no obligation to purchase any books as explained on the back of this card.

340 SDL D7ZT   240 SDL D7ZK

FIRST NAME	LAST NAME

ADDRESS

APT.#	CITY

STATE/PROV.	ZIP/POSTAL CODE

(S-IM-06/05)

7	**7**	**7**	Worth TWO FREE BOOKS plus a BONUS Mystery Gift!
🍒	🍒	🍒	Worth TWO FREE BOOKS!
🔔	🔔	♣	TRY AGAIN!

www.eHarlequin.com

sagging couch. Not at the far end, as she had in the past few days, but right next to him. He was just as surprised when she reached for the remote on the coffee table and turned off the television.

"We need to talk."

"No good ever followed a woman uttering that sentence," he said. *"Ever."*

Tess actually smiled, a little. "Well, I won't be breaking the rules, then. I don't think you're going to like what I have to say."

"Uh-oh. Are you kicking me out?" Odd, that being thrown off her lumpy couch was the worst scenario he could think of, at the moment.

"No. I want you to send Mangino home."

That was not what he'd expected to hear. "I can't do that."

"At least tell him that sleeping with Serena is not part of the job, and he needs to find a way to end it so that it won't turn ugly," she said almost sharply. "She likes him, Flynn, she likes him a lot. And when this is all over and she realizes that getting close to her was a part of the job, it's going to break her heart."

"Loomis doesn't strike me as the kind of woman whose heart is easily broken."

"Looks can be deceiving," Tess said softly, not quite as frantic as she had been, but not pacified, either. "Really, Flynn. I can't believe you had one of your men seduce a woman just to…"

"Whoa," he interrupted her. "That was *not* part of the plan. I never told Dante to sleep with Loomis, and I don't believe it was part of his plan, either. It just kinda happened."

"Just kinda happened?" she repeated in disbelief. "Give me a break. They have been involved almost since the moment y'all arrived, and they haven't slowed down yet. You expect me to believe it just *happened?*"

He was a heartbeat away from losing his temper, and from telling Tess that Loomis had been the one to seduce Dante, not the other way around. That didn't much matter at this point, anyway. Didn't she get it? "Sometimes things don't go the way you intended, no matter how careful you are. I didn't intend to like you, but here I am sleeping on this damned couch because I don't want you to be here alone and you won't leave, as any woman with a lick of common sense would." Flynn leaned closer to Tess, intent on intimidating her. "Let me tell you how screwed up this job is," he said softly. "It's not just Dante's love life that's twisted. I'd rather let Austin go than take even the *remotest* chance that you or one of the kids would get in the way. I'm sitting here trying to figure out how to get all the girls and you away from here before Saturday morning, and even if it means scaring Austin away, I'll do it. I should be sitting in front of a computer analyzing data I've already seen a hundred times just in case I might see something new, and instead I'm here, watching a basketball game when I freakin' hate basketball, and wondering if there's any chance…any chance at all…that one of these nights I'm going to end up *not* sleeping on the damned couch!"

When he stopped to take a deep breath, Tess laid one

soft hand on his cheek. The hand stopped everything else he had to say, just like that. She drifted in and up, slowly moving to him, and then she kissed him. It had been days since she'd kissed him, and dammit—he'd missed it. He'd missed it more than he'd imagined he could miss anything.

The kiss deepened, Tess's arms snaked around his neck, and he held her close. For a moment he was caught up in the sensation of falling—falling hard, falling head first into a place he had avoided for a long time. Her mouth was so sweet, and it opened to him in a way he had not expected.

She kissed like a woman who was scared but ready.

Her body fit against his just so, small and curvy and soft, as if it had been made to be right here, right now. He did what he'd been thinking about for days; he tested those curves with the palm of his hand. There was something so delicate and rare and beautiful about a woman's curves. Her hip, her waist, her breasts. While he touched he drew in Tess's heat and her softness, he breathed in her scent and tasted her mouth with his lips and his tongue, until she moved that mouth from his, slow and easy.

Tess rested her forehead to his shoulder and ran her thumb along the side of his neck. "Still sore?"

"No."

She shifted a little, moving in closer. "It's sleeping on the couch that did it, you know."

"Yeah, I know."

"Maybe you shouldn't sleep on the couch anymore."

He nodded slightly, and thrust his fingers through her

thick, auburn hair to hold her more tightly against him. He had a hard-on that wasn't going away anytime soon, thanks to that kiss. Staying here, close to Tess, was going to be torture.

"The floor's not so bad," he said. "I've slept in worse places, believe me. I can always move back into the hall, if this is getting too weird for you. Or I can get out of here and have one of the guys on patrol in the hallway. We can make it work, somehow, so I'm not underfoot. I'll just…get out of your hair."

Tess lifted her head and looked him in the eye. Well, he'd been wrong about one thing; she wasn't scared.

"Or not," she whispered, and then she kissed him again.

She liked the way Flynn made her feel when he kissed her, or held her, or let it slip that he cared about her in a way that was not at all meaningless or casual. They didn't have a future. Until she knew what was going to happen with Laura she couldn't plan any kind of future with anyone. But she wanted this, for tonight.

Coming to Flynn, sitting beside him and making it clear what she wanted, hadn't been easy for her. But it had felt so natural. So right.

"I don't have any kind of…" she paused and took a deep breath. She wanted Flynn, and she was letting him know it, and still she couldn't say the word "condom."

"I do," he said. "Two."

Two. Good. She still wanted kids, one day, but not with a man who wouldn't be here a week from now, casual or not, and not until she was settled in another place…with Laura or without her.

Flynn didn't jump off the couch and lead her into the bedroom, as soon as she made it clear what she wanted. Instead he kissed her again, as he held her close against his hard body. She allowed herself to touch him, in a way she had not been able to before. She pressed her palm to his chest, his arm, his side. He was solid, the muscle tight and ridged. He was constructed of angles and sharp edges, instead of gentle curves. But he was warm, and his heart beat fast and strong.

He touched her while they kissed, slipping one hand beneath her blouse to caress bare skin. His fingers worked against her flesh, his thumb raked along a rib as if he were memorizing it. A rhythm set in. The sway of his fingers, the motion of his tongue, their breathing, their heartbeats. Deep inside, where she had been sleeping for so long, something came to life. It fluttered and grasped, demanding more.

She slipped her fingers beneath Flynn's shirt to stroke bare skin, and she felt his response, as muscles tightened and the kiss deepened. He wanted her—he had always wanted her, in a very basic way. She'd seen it in his eyes, and now she felt it.

When he took his mouth from hers and moved the kisses to her neck, she tilted her head to give him better access, closing her eyes and drinking in the sensations. Beneath her ear, along the column of her throat where neck turned to shoulder, he tasted it all. She

melted beneath him, she breathed differently and
reached for more and savored every new sensation.

And then it was her turn, and she twisted into a new
position where she could suck gently against Flynn's
throat. He tasted like a man, of sweat and soap and skin.
While she kissed his throat, he caressed her breasts
through the thin blouse she wore, then with nothing between his hand and her skin but a plain bra. She pushed
his shirt up and laid both palms against a tight stomach,
where muscles rippled and she felt the occasional quiver
that matched her own. She lowered her head and kissed
that hard stomach, and felt the rippling against her lips
as he reacted.

Her blouse came off, quickly and efficiently whipped
over her head, and Flynn kissed the swell of her breasts.
Those lips against her skin made her shake, and that was
before he unfastened her bra and tossed it aside to lay
those lips over the sensitive nipples.

Her reaction was unexpectedly intense, and her back
arched to bring Flynn closer. He responded by suckling
one nipple deep into that warm mouth and unfastening
her jeans. His tongue flickered against a nipple while
he slowly lowered her zipper. Her insides clenched, and
a small, unintentional sound escaped from low in her
throat.

She was stretched out on the couch, with Flynn's
mouth on one breast and his hand slithering down her
unzipped jeans. Tess held her breath, waiting for him to
touch her. Waiting and shaking and flying.

Her jeans slipped lower, and then his hand was there,

between her legs, finding and caressing the nub at her entrance, stroking in a rhythm that matched the way he suckled her nipple. She wanted tell him to stop, to undress, to take her into the bedroom where a big, soft bed waited. But she was incapable of saying a word. Her hips rocked against his caress, and she couldn't think of anything else.

He urged her legs farther apart, and then his fingers were inside her. A sharp sensation knifed through her body, and she swayed into him. And then she came so hard she cried out loud and held Flynn's head in her hands while she quivered and lurched.

Flynn kissed her on the mouth, almost gentle once again as he eased her into a sitting position. She felt boneless and shaken. Half-dressed and contented and decadently happy.

And not yet finished.

"Can we go to bed, now?" she whispered.

"Whatever you want, Red." Flynn stood and helped her to her feet, and then he lifted her straight off the ground, carrying her that way toward the bedroom.

"I want to see you naked," she said with a smile.

"You got it."

"I want to make you as crazy as you make me."

"Already there," he said as they entered the darkened bedroom.

"No, I don't think so."

He set her on her feet beside the bed, where he kissed her again and slipped his hands into the loosened waistband of her jeans and panties, pushing them both to the floor in a long, gentle motion. She stepped out of them, so that she stood naked before him. She had always been shy, but tonight she wasn't. She didn't know why, and didn't care. Maybe because Flynn so obviously liked what he saw…whether she was wearing a shapeless white uniform or nothing at all.

She unfastened his jeans, and lowered the zipper. He didn't help; he just stood there and watched her with those blue eyes of his. When the zipper was down she slipped her hand inside and palmed his erection, testing the length and the thickness and the heat of it, claiming it as her own, at least for tonight. Touching him made her clench again, it made her want to grasp what she felt in an entirely different and more intimate way.

She'd given all her adult life to her sick father, her lost daughter, the husband she'd never been able to satisfy and the lack of family that had left her feeling incomplete. She felt as if she'd never taken the time to do anything for herself. She wasn't selfish, she just didn't often think about what *she* wanted and needed.

Tonight that was changing. Flynn was just for her. They had no expectations, no plans, no needs beyond the moment. She liked it, more than she'd imagined she could.

Before she lowered his jeans, Flynn reached into his back pocket and withdrew a wallet. Inside that wallet were two condoms, which he carelessly tossed onto the bed before whipping off his shirt and helping her to finish getting rid of the pants. By the time they fell into the bed, he was as naked as she was, and just as anxious for what was to come.

But like before, he didn't rush. Tess lay on her back, looking up at him, and he studied her face while one hand raked down her side and over her hip in a possessive manner.

"See what I mean?" he said softly. "Every now and then things you don't plan on just happen."

"Good things," she whispered.

"Sometimes." And then he kissed her throat, sending chills through her entire body. He kissed his way down her arm. Neck, shoulder, inner elbow, wrist. Tess closed her eyes and melted. No man had ever made love to her this way, and she was blindsided by the physical pleasure Flynn offered her. She'd wanted him before tonight, she'd been thinking about this for days, but she'd never dreamed it would be this good.

She caressed his length, then trailed her fingers along his taut belly, then she touched his erection again. He quivered. She hadn't thought she could make a man like Flynn quiver, just with the touch of one hand. He moaned once, then moved away from her, so she could no longer reach him.

He kissed her belly, as she had kissed his earlier when they'd been sitting on the couch, only he stayed longer at the task. He held her hips in his hands and raked his thumbs against her hipbone while he trailed his tongue across tender flesh that had never been kissed before, while he feathered little kisses all over her body until she felt as if she were floating off the bed.

Finally he spread her thighs with large, warm hands, caressing her gently and then hard. She closed her eyes and rocked against him. Already she was anxious for him, and this time she wanted it all. She wanted him inside her, completely and deeply inside her. Now. He reached for one of the condoms, and she heard the soft tear of a foil package.

And then a moment later he was there, pushing against her. She opened for him, her body arched and clenched and surged, and Flynn was finally a part of her.

He moved slowly, as if starting all over again. The rhythmic sway of his hips didn't take him deep, but teased them both with shallow thrusts that soon had her breathless. Once he surged deep and she gasped. And then he went back to that gentle motion.

She closed her eyes, moved with him, and forgot everything and everyone that existed beyond this bed.

It was a good moment, a time of pleasure and affection and passion. There was power in this bed, in the physical act of her and Flynn joining together and in the emotional release it took to bring them here. She wanted to keep him here, just this way, for a long, long time.

When he started to move faster and deeper, she met each sway with one of her own, and when he buried himself deep inside her, her body reacted fiercely. She cried out as the orgasm made her clench around him. He came hard, too. She felt it, even as her own release continued on waves that danced through her body from head to toe.

Then things were gentle again, and the world came back, and she drew Flynn down to her. And he came, drifting down slowly.

She wondered if he had ever considered that falling in love was one of those things that sometimes just happened.

Chapter 8

Since he was resting in a soft bed with a beautiful woman beside him, instead of on a lumpy couch that was more than a foot too short, he should be sleeping like a baby. But instead of sleeping, Flynn stared at the ceiling and listened to Tess breathe.

After the life he'd planned for himself had fallen apart and he'd buried his wife and his baby, he'd shut down completely, for a while. No women, no close friends, nothing but work. The Marines, then the Benning Agency. A couple of years after the accident…dammit, his entire life was divided into before and after and there was no getting around it…he'd tried casual sex. He hadn't much cared for it, past the obvious fun part, so he'd eventually settled for the only choice left for a man who didn't have a wife….

He hooked up with women who were just like him. Women who weren't looking for commitment or a relationship, just a semiregular sexual partner who wouldn't ask for much in return. Women who wouldn't cry when you got tired of them. Women who didn't want more than he had to give. Women who were just as afraid of hearing those three little words as he was.

Tess wanted more than that. She hadn't said so, not yet, but she was the kind of woman who would want everything. Commitment, promises, companionship beyond the bedroom. She'd want heart and soul, as well as body, and he didn't have that left to give. He'd buried his heart and soul along with his wife and his little girl, and he didn't think he could get them back even if he wanted to.

In sleep she sidled up against him, sighed and settled her naked body against his as if she belonged there. The really bad thing was…

Maybe she did.

He rolled on his side to face Tess, drew the covers all the way down, and laid his hand on her stomach, just below her belly button. Her skin was so soft, so tender and fine and unlike his tough hide, he couldn't keep his hands off her. She was like that on the inside, too. Gentle. Vulnerable. Too good for a man who didn't intend to stay any longer than he had to. He'd known that all along, so why was he still drawn to her? Why was he here?

Tess slept with a dim night-light, in case she had to get up in the night. Maybe she was afraid of the dark, of the unknown, of things she couldn't see. He could see her well enough, even though the shadows were deep and pockets of darkness filled the corners of the room. If anything, the faint light made her look too perfect. Too fine to be real. Every curve was perfection, pale and smooth and gently shaped.

She was so beautiful, and he wanted her again.

"It's a little cold to be sleeping with no covers," Tess said without opening her eyes.

"I can warm you up."

She smiled and his heart hitched, and that was a *very* bad thing. "I'm sure you can."

He ran his hand up her inner thigh, and when he touched her she opened for him. One touch, and she was ready. One stroke, and she sighed. In that sigh there was contentment, and invitation, and pleasure. In one soft sigh, he heard too much. He heard everything he didn't want.

Flynn grabbed the last condom from the bedside table, and quickly sheathed himself. He rolled atop Tess, and gently spread her thighs wider apart with his knee.

"No kissing this time?" she asked in a soft and dreamy voice as he pushed inside her. She took a deep breath as he held himself there, arched her back and sighed, content for the moment.

"Do you want kissing?"

"Always," she whispered. He pushed deeper, and it seemed that she drew him inside. Her hips rose to meet him. "You're so good at it. I never knew kissing was an art until I met you."

He kissed her, for a long moment, while he barely

moved inside her. Her mouth opened beneath his, sleepy and sensuous and inviting. When the kiss was done Tess wrapped her legs around his hips, and her body moved sharply against his. For a woman who had been so reluctant and suspicious when they'd met, she responded with an abandon that mystified him. She was a passionate woman, with fire and spirit…and heart. That heart was in everything she did, it was in everything she touched. Heart was evident in the way she made love, in the way her body responded to his, and her fingers explored him, and her legs wrapped around his, and her breath came in that way that told him she was almost there.

She arched her back to draw him deeper, and threw her head back as she pulsed around him and gave one sharp cry, as if she were surprised by the quickness and the intensity of the orgasm. Her body lurched, her hands grasped for him, her bare body and his were pressed together, sweating on a cool February night. And then he forgot everything else but the way Tess felt wrapped around him, hot and tight and clenching, and his own release came while she still shuddered around him.

She made a moaning, purring sound of contentment as he kissed her again, and she wrapped her arms around his neck. Her tongue teased his, she was open and embracing beneath him. When the kiss ended, her fingers lazily raked through the short strands of his hair. For a moment, he thought she was going to say something…something important, something momentous. Something he didn't want to hear. But in the end, she said nothing at all, and Flynn was relieved.

He liked Tess. He even cared about her, in the only way that he could.

But he didn't want her heart and all the obligations that would come with it.

The new occupants of the men's dormitory were definitely up to no good. It was a complication, but nothing Dale couldn't handle. In fact, it made a simple job all the more challenging. They were not smarter, they were not better at their vocation.

But a diversion was called for. Something big. Something that would stop them in their tracks. Killing a student was momentarily tempting, but it was also distasteful. There were unspoken rules to this game, and Dale always played by the rules.

Well, most of them. Some rules were made to be broken, but the idea of killing a child was still loathsome.

Anyone who made the mistake of getting involved with the interlopers was fair game, however. That too was one of the rules. Dale knew too well that nothing stopped a macho man in his tracks any quicker than finding the woman with whom he was sleeping dead.

For the first time in a long time, it was the alarm clock that woke Tess. Usually she was up at least fifteen minutes before it went off, but not today. After all that had happened last night, she wasn't surprised that she'd overslept. She hit the snooze button, drew up the covers, and turned over to discover that the other side of the bed was empty. Flynn was apparently already awake and about.

She didn't smell coffee or hear him moving in the other room. The bathroom door was open, and he wasn't in there, either. Was he sleeping on the couch again?

Her heart thudded at the thought. Last night had been very special, for her. She didn't trust easily, especially where men were concerned. She certainly didn't invite a man into her bed on a whim. She hadn't even allowed herself to consider that it might not be just as special for Flynn. After all, he said one-night stands were pathetic. He did care about her. He obviously found her physically appealing.

Obviously.

She was actually a little sore this morning, but then she hadn't been with a man since her marriage had ended, and that had been…years. Too long. Yeah, it had been a long time. Had she forgotten how good sex could be? Or had it just never been this good before? Heaven above, sore or not she wanted Flynn again. The man was positively addictive.

Grabbing her bathrobe, she stepped into the living room. No, Flynn wasn't on the couch. Maybe he was checking out the storeroom, or maybe he'd gotten a phone call and he hadn't wanted to wake her up. She didn't think anything was wrong. He would have awakened her and told her, if that was the case.

Certain that everything was fine in her little world, she took a quick shower, and brushed her teeth, and dressed in her uniform. For the first time, she wished her wardrobe was different. Sexier. More eye-catching. She wanted Flynn to think she was pretty, and wasn't that unexpected. Somewhere among the things she'd packed away before taking this job she had a number of pretty dresses. High heels. Heaven above, at this moment if Stephanie McCabe offered her a makeover, she'd probably take it.

When she placed her toothpaste in the mirrored medicine cabinet, she stared at the box of hair dye sitting there. Dark honey brown. Looking at that box snapped her back to reality, unfortunately. If Flynn canceled parents' day, she wouldn't need to use the hair color, but if the day went off as planned she'd spend the weekend as a brunette. The odds that Jack would recognize her were slim, she knew that, but she couldn't take the chance.

He probably wouldn't lower himself to look a cafeteria employee in the face. He'd consider it beneath him to acknowledge someone in such a lowly position. Jack was such a snob, just like his mother. Why hadn't she seen that before it was too late?

If he did look at her, it was possible he wouldn't even recognize her after thirteen years. Still, brown hair would make her more anonymous, and for this coming weekend she definitely wanted to be anonymous. She wanted to be able to get close enough to Jack to discern for herself that he was a good father. And if he wasn't…

Last night Flynn had made her forget about the dilemma that had brought her here, and she wasn't complaining. It had been great. It had been fabulous. But she hadn't come here to find Flynn. She'd come here to get to know her daughter. Flynn Benning couldn't be anything more than a momentary indulgence…but oh, what an indulgence last night had been. She couldn't be sorry.

He still wasn't back, when it was time to go downstairs and get breakfast started. She'd see him there, she supposed, but it was disappointing to start the day without a kiss, or two. She opened the door, engaged the lock and almost came face-to-face with Coach Calhoun. Cal, Flynn called him.

"Oh." She stepped back in surprise. "Is something wrong?"

"No, ma'am," he answered in a calm, emotionless voice.

It was very clear to Tess that Cal was on guard duty.

"Where's Flynn?" she asked, suddenly worried. Something must've happened to call him away so early.

"Major Benning is in his quarters, ma'am."

"Stop calling me ma'am," she said as she passed him and headed for the stairs. "Makes me feel old, and I don't think I'm even as old as you are."

He followed her. "Yes, ma—" He grunted softly. "Okay."

"Cal, right?" she asked as she hurried down the stairs.

"That'll do."

"How long have you been on guard duty, Cal?"

He hesitated before answering, then said, "About three hours."

Tess didn't look back, even though the answer surprised her. If Cal had been in the hallway for three hours, then Flynn had left her apartment almost directly after the second time they'd made love.

Maybe she wasn't so special after all.

* * *

He'd been at the Frances Teague Academy for two weeks, and it felt like a lifetime. He wasn't a teacher, he didn't even like kids, and there was no guarantee that Austin was going to show up here, not on Saturday, not ever. For all they knew he had a daughter and he'd been checking out boarding schools, in his own special way. It was a scary thought, that maybe Austin wasn't here to kill one of the parents, but was in fact a parent himself. Or herself. Flynn still had a hard time with the idea of a woman as a hired killer, though he knew it had happened before and would happen again.

"Mr. Benning, Mr. Benning, Mr. Benning." Laura's hand fluttered and her fingers danced. "Shouldn't we have the grades back on the papers we turned in last week? Mr. Hill always has our work back to us in three or four days, at the most."

Of course it was her, that pesky kid he liked, for some reason he couldn't quite put his finger on. He couldn't very well tell her that he wasn't qualified to grade papers, and that when Mr. Hill got back from his sick leave he'd handle that job himself. "Next week," he answered. "Maybe."

Most of the girls didn't care about their grades, not today. The last day of February was an unusually warm one. The sun was shining, and the trees believed spring was not only coming, it was here. They seemed brighter today, the branches livelier and the buds greener. Half the class was staring out the window.

"Today we're going over the vocabulary," he said, reverting to Hill's regular if unimaginative lesson plan. His eyes were drawn to the windows, himself. "And we're having class outside."

"Mr. Hill never—" Laura began.

"Mr. Hill's not here," Flynn interrupted, before the girl could finish her protest. "And I feel cooped up in here today." He didn't want to consider that it wasn't the weather that made him feel like he wanted to escape. Tess had been on his mind since he'd left her sleeping. He had never intended to hurt her, to be a jerk, to run in the night like a coward.

But the alternative was to stay, to get closer to her than he'd intended, to draw her into his life in a way that would be hard—if not impossible—to shake.

The students took their books and filed out of the classroom, some of them smiling, others confused. Outside the redbrick building, the fresh air did clear Flynn's mind some. But it didn't chase Tess out.

He pointed to an ancient live oak tree, and the girls headed in that direction. They were beginning to get into the spirit of things, and some of them actually skipped. Laura and Bev slowed down, and before he knew what was happening they bracketed him.

Surrounded by the enemy.

"I didn't see you at breakfast," Laura said brightly.

"I overslept."

"Is that why you're so grumpy?" the usually quiet Bev asked, her voice as low and tentative as usual.

"I'm not grumpy!" Flynn barked. Both girls moved

slightly away from him. "Okay, I'm a little grumpy," he conceded.

"I like having class outside," Bev said, obviously anxious to change the subject away from her irritable history teacher's mood. "Usually we're only outside walking to one building or another or to walk the track in the afternoon or for soccer practice. I didn't like soccer much at first, but I like it now. Did you know that Coach Calhoun has been teaching us self-defense?"

"He has?"

"Yeah," Laura said brightly. "He said every woman, even a small one, needs to know how to fight, and that we would probably never need to know, but if we did it was a good idea to have a few tricks up our sleeves."

"Coach Calhoun is a smart guy," Flynn said. Surely Cal looked at these girls and thought of his sister Kelly, and wondered if things would have been different for her if she'd had a few tricks up her sleeve. Here he'd been mooning over how hard being stuck at this all-girls' school was for him, when it had to be just as hard for Cal. Maybe harder. His sister was still out there, somewhere, scared and running and alone, and he didn't know if he'd ever find her.

If Sadie had her way, that reunion would come soon. Since she was pregnant and her husband refused to let her go on any assignment that might turn out to be dangerous, she'd committed herself full-time to finding Kelly Calhoun. On the computer, on the phone, even on the road now and then…she searched.

The girls sat beneath the limbs of the oak tree, and

Flynn paced. He had the students take turns reading from the book and going over the vocabulary words. After a few minutes, Flynn felt as if he were seconds from drifting into welcome sleep. The textbook made for boring reading, dates and names and places all strung together in a way that was dull as ditch water.

Halfway through one particularly long and uninteresting sentence that was being read in a droning voice by an indifferent student, Flynn slammed his book shut with a force that made half the girls jump.

"Okay, who thinks this is boring?"

A few tentative hands went up, then a few more. After Flynn raised his hand, all the others joined in.

"This book is mostly crap. History isn't about dates and numbers and new words, it's about people. It's about girls like you who lived through periods of change. Change brought about by war, and technological advances, and politics. Day-to-day life is what's interesting about history. Do you think everyone who lived back then was pompous and white-haired?"

He kept talking. Flynn Benning had always been good at talking, especially when he got on a roll. Today he was on a roll. Before he knew it the girls had their books closed, and they were watching him with wide, young, interested eyes. And for a while he forgot about Tess, and Austin, and Cal's sister and everything else.

They were all surprised when the bell to change classes rang, and the girls scrambled up and ran toward the building. Some of them were smiling. Flynn was not. Just because he'd actually enjoyed teaching today, that didn't mean he'd lost his edge.

He followed behind the students at a distance, until he ran into Serena Loomis, who was headed into the building for her first class.

"Dr. Barber doesn't allow classes to be held outside," Loomis said with a touch of bitterness.

"Dr. Barber can kiss my…"

"Now, let's don't go there," she interrupted. "I know you're just a sub, but it's not wise to piss off Dr. Barber. She's a tough old bird."

"Tell me about it," Flynn muttered.

Tess had asked him to see that Dante ended his relationship with Loomis now, so she wouldn't get hurt later. The math teacher was pretty tough herself, she was distant and cynical. Was it even possible that she was capable of getting emotionally involved with her lover?

More importantly, was it possible that she was working with the killer they were looking for? Her credentials and her fingerprints checked out, but they didn't have much on her that was personal. Loomis didn't have much of a social life and never had, from what they'd discovered about her. Dante was certain she was clean as a whistle, but Dante hadn't been thinking with his brain for a good long while, now, not where Serena Loomis was concerned.

"I didn't mean to snap. I've had a bad day, and it's still early."

"Tell me about it," she answered softly.

At the building entrance, they stopped. Inside they

could see girls moving from one classroom to the other, shuffling books and notebooks and fiddling with their hair or their clothes. They were bright, in more ways than one, and they were special. Each and every one of them.

"Tess Stafford is a nice woman," Loomis said, looking up at Flynn with dark eyes that were fearless, behind those dark-rimmed glasses. Fearless, but not emotionless. "It's really not admirable of you to come here for a temporary gig and sweep her off her feet when we all know you're not going to stay. As soon as Mr. Hill and all the others have recovered, they'll come back and you and the other temps will be gone, and everything will go back to normal. So don't jerk her around, okay?"

Too late.

Was she talking about Tess or herself? And how did she know he'd jerked Tess around? For all he knew, the women had spent the morning comparing notes, and wasn't *that* a scary thought.

"Are you two close friends?" Flynn asked, as he reached past Loomis and opened the door for her to enter the building. The hallway was almost empty now, the girls in their respective classes. "Is that why you're trying to warn me off?"

"We're not close friends," Loomis said, a touch of hostility in her voice. "That doesn't mean I can't think she's a good person who doesn't need to be stepped on."

Flynn's heart did a sick flip as Serena Loomis walked briskly to her classroom, leaving him behind. Tess was a good person, and he didn't think there was any way for him to go back and undo what he'd already done. He'd screwed up big time, and no matter what Tess said or thought about him…he had a deep, sick feeling that he couldn't fix this one.

Chapter 9

Tess walked briskly around the track, trying to burn off some of the energy that bubbled up inside her. Energy and embarrassment and anger. She might be naive, but she wasn't stupid. Flynn had missed breakfast *and* lunch, and in her mind the initial presumption that he regretted what had happened last night was confirmed.

As she walked, Tess tried to tell herself that his withdrawal was for the best. She didn't have time in her life for a man, not when Laura's situation was still unsettled. It didn't matter how tempting Flynn was or how good he made her feel, she didn't have time for him. Not now. Besides, she wanted more kids one day, no matter what happened with Laura. Flynn was adamant that he did not. She'd always known that he was a temporary

fixture here, at the school and in her life. So why were
her feelings hurt?

She increased her gait, trying to work off her frus-
tration. Her feelings were hurt because like it or not,
Flynn touched a place inside her that she had thought
long dead, and she'd enjoyed it. More than that, she'd
reveled in it. He made her feel as if her life were full
again, as if there was more to the days to come than pain
and regret. There could also be laughter and pleasure,
and the warmth that came from lying beside someone
who made you wonder if maybe love really did exist,
in its purest sense.

Flynn had never mentioned love and neither had she,
but last night she had definitely allowed the four-letter
word to cross her mind a time or two. How could she not?

On the soccer field in the center of the track, the high
school team practiced. They'd play a game against the
local high school on Saturday afternoon, right after the
middle school teams played. It was a part of parents'
day. From what she'd heard, in the past those games had
usually not gone well. Maybe with Cal as coach things
would be different.

Tess stopped for a moment and turned her attention
to the girls on the field while she caught her breath. It
was supposed to be practice, but the girls weren't playing soccer or running one of the drills their new coach
had been using to get them in better shape. They were
all lined up, in an orderly and very quiet row. The students were watching Cal and Dante Mangino, and at
first Tess thought the two men were fighting. In slow

motion. Then she realized, with a heavy thump of her heart, what they were doing.

They were teaching the girls to fight.

She should be outraged, but instead she felt a sense of relief. Flynn's men were taking care of these girls in the only way they knew how.

Maybe *those guys* weren't always so bad, after all.

He was too freakin' old to feel this way—nervous and uncertain, as if he was about to ask a pretty girl out for the first time, and he wasn't sure what her answer would be.

Everyone else had left the main building, even Mary Jo, when Flynn walked into the dining hall. Tess was cleaning the kitchen with a vengeance; he heard the slamming of pots and dishes from the doorway between the hallway and the dining hall. For a moment, he stopped and reconsidered what he was about to do. Tess was pissed, and rightly so.

But he was a grown man, not a kid, and he could take his medicine if the situation called for it. Besides, he was starving.

Tess didn't hear him walk into the kitchen, so he was able to watch her for a moment. Yeah, she was angry. The way she slung those dishes around, it was a wonder the floor wasn't littered with broken crockery. Of course, the night was still young.

"Flynn is actually my middle name," he said, in a voice just loud enough to carry over the clang of dishes.

Tess spun around quickly, surprised. She held a wet plate in one hand, and a dishrag in the other. "What?"

"Flynn is my middle name."

Her surprise faded, and a mask of anger dropped over her pretty face. "And what makes you think this should concern me?"

He took a step toward her, moving into the kitchen. Tess all but bristled.

"My mother watched an old movie marathon while she was in labor, and then the drugs kicked in, I guess. Anyway, instead of John William Benning III, she decided to name me after the actor she had watched on TV all day."

Tess's eyes actually widened, a little. "She didn't."

"Errol Flynn Benning," he said. "There you go, Red, my deepest, darkest secret. None of the guys know."

She didn't smile, and there was no softening of her eyes.

"I guess it could be worse," he said as he came to a halt several feet away. "She could've named me Robin Hood or Captain Blood."

For a moment, she looked as if she didn't know what to say. Some of the anger in her eyes faded.

"What do you want?" Tess asked in a slightly less acrimonious voice. "If you're hungry, just say so."

"I'm hungry," he said softly.

Tess turned away and headed for the refrigerator, a monster of an appliance that took up almost one wall of the kitchen.

"I'm hungry, but that's not the only reason I'm here," Flynn said. "I'm not a kid who runs away from my mistakes."

"Can't prove it by me," Tess muttered as she rummaged in the fridge. Flynn watched her as she pulled out the makings for a sandwich, put it all together, and slapped the finished product onto a plate. She walked to him and handed him the plate on an outstretched arm, as if she didn't want to get too close. "Eat in here. I've already cleaned the dining hall and I'd rather not have to do it again."

After she walked away, he placed the plate on an already cleaned counter. "We need to talk," he said.

"No good ever came of a man saying those words," Tess answered without turning to face him. She continued to rinse plates and place them in the industrial-size dishwasher.

Maybe it would be easier to leave things this way. Anger was a healthy emotion. Tess would stay pissed for a while, and then he'd leave, and eventually all would be well again. She'd just remember the way their unexpected relationship had ended, not the spectacular way it had begun.

Why the hell didn't he believe that? It would make things so much easier.

"I can't get involved with you," he said starkly. He didn't think it would help matters any if he told her that he was in danger of liking her too much.

"You've already made that clear," she answered, again without so much as glancing his way. "Very clear, in fact."

He should let it go, he knew that, and in the past he had been great at letting things go. Nothing mattered, beyond the moment and the job. But he couldn't just let this go.

"You're a great lady, I mean that, but from now on I'm going to have Cal on duty in the building at night." Cal had never needed much sleep anyway. He would grab a nap beforehand, and a couple of hours in the morning before he was needed on the soccer field, and that would do until this job was over. Just a few more days, if they were lucky. "I'm going to stick around for a couple of hours, and then he'll relieve me until morning."

"You can leave now, for all I care," she said sharply. "I'd rather take my chances with your thief."

If he'd believed that assertion, it would have made him angry. Not that he thought Tess should be happy to have him around. But she didn't need to take chances with her life.

"A thief who kills people," he clarified.

"Whatever," she muttered. She slung a plate around, and he expected it to hit the floor or the wall—or him—at any moment. It didn't.

Tess should live to be old and gray, and have lots of kids, and make brownies and cookies for her own children. She deserved to have a husband who would love and appreciate her and be home every night, a husband who would gladly give her the family she wanted. He couldn't be that guy—he didn't have it in him anymore.

"I think I'll stick around until Cal gets here."

Flynn stood at the counter and ate. Hungry as he was, it was tough to choke the sandwich down. What a day this had been. First of all, the fiasco with Tess. He wasn't supposed to look at her and see more than a woman to have some fun with, he wasn't supposed to feel obligated and attached and needy, where she was concerned. Then another fiasco—he'd actually enjoyed teaching class today. The girls had listened to him, and they'd asked questions. Teaching was supposed to be a cover, that's all, and in the beginning he had hated the classroom.

He liked his life as it was, as it had become. He lived without complication, without obligations beyond getting the jobs he was hired to do done. No kids, no woman, no family to worry about. No plans beyond the next job, no worries about what might happen if that job went wrong. He didn't worry, because it didn't matter. Nothing mattered that much anymore.

Somewhere along that line of thought, Flynn lost his appetite. He ended up eating half the sandwich and throwing the other half away. Then he handed the plate to Tess, and she jerked it from his hand. In a way he wished she would throw it against the wall, or against him. Maybe it would make him feel better.

But she didn't throw anything. "I thought you said one-night stands were pathetic."

"They are," he grumbled. "Apparently I'm a more pathetic guy than I realized."

She shook her head and made a disgusted huffing noise. "You are pathetic," she agreed. "And a coward to boot. You couldn't stick around this morning and tell me yourself that what happened was a mistake? You had to avoid me all day to make your point? You really didn't need to worry. I never intended to cling to you or cry when I found out what happened didn't mean anything other than a quick—"

"That's not true," Flynn said hotly. The problem was that it *did* mean something, not that he could tell her that. "I'm here on an assignment, and sleeping with you wasn't a part of the plan. It was unprofessional and I apologize."

She turned to look at him, straight on. "What happened didn't have anything to do with your job here, and we both know it." Her anger faded, some. Her lips and her eyes softened.

There was a part of him that wanted to tell her he'd be back when the job was over to see if what they had would work beyond this moment...but there was the bigger problem of the life she deserved; the life he couldn't give her.

Very faintly, very distant, Flynn heard the front door of the building being unlocked. Cal was supposed to be catching a nap before coming on duty, and no one else should be here. How tough would it be for Austin to get a key to the building?

He drew a small gun from his ankle holster, and looked Tess in the eye. "Stay here." She looked at the gun with newly widened, and newly frightened, eyes. She'd seen it before, but its sudden appearance tonight surprised her. Good. She needed to know who he really was. Maybe it would keep her angry.

Flynn was halfway through the dining hall, gun in hand, when a familiar voice called out a friendly and unconcerned, "It's just me."

By the time Cal walked into the room Flynn's gun was reholstered, tucked out of sight. Tess had not been happy to see it, and she'd expect an explanation. Later, maybe. Maybe not. "You're early," he said, and then he saw that Cal was not alone. His wife, Livvie, was with him, and she wore a smile so wide it likely couldn't be scrubbed off.

"I'm here to beg off guard duty," Cal said. "I hate to, but Livvie's just here for the night and I'd rather not spend it in the hall. I'll talk to Murphy about coming in tonight…."

"No. I'll stick around." Crap, he should have known something would come up to ruin his cowardly plan. Cal was a hardened agent who Flynn trusted with Tess's life. Murphy was too damn green, and Dante was too damn distracted by the math teacher.

Tess heard voices and stuck her head into the room. Livvie continued to smile, as she headed in Tess's direction. "I'm going to see if I can rustle up a glass of milk or maybe some ice cream. Besides, you two need to talk."

Crap again. No good ever came of those words….

Flynn sat at the nearest table, and Cal took the chair across from him. There was something different about the man, tonight. Something that made Flynn's heart sink. Cal was elated and terrified and confused and content, all at once. And Livvie's smile—Flynn had seen a very similar one once before, a long time ago. He was about to lose his best man; he knew that before Cal opened his mouth.

"Livvie's pregnant," Cal said. "She went to the doctor this morning and he confirmed it. Since it was just a couple hours drive she decided to come over and tell me in person." He looked very uncomfortable. "Apparently she wanted to see my face when I heard the news."

Flynn's heart skipped a beat, even though he had expected as much, thanks to Livvie's smile and her unusual request for a glass of milk. She was usually a coffee drinker, even at night. "Congratulations." First Sadie and now this. Just what he needed, to be surrounded on all sides by pregnant women. Even after all these years the very thought terrified him.

"Thanks." Cal actually squirmed in his seat. "I'm going to have to quit my job. Livvie didn't ask me to," he added quickly. "But I don't want to leave her for weeks at a time anymore, and I don't want to put my life on the line for someone else when I've got a family at home."

Quinn Calhoun, a family man. He never would've thought it possible. "Makes sense, I suppose, but we'll miss you. When do you plan to leave?"

"After this job. We've got some money saved, and I want to look for Kelly full-time for a few months."

"We'll help with that," Flynn said. "You still have the full resources of the Benning Agency at your disposal. Whatever you need, Cal, it's yours."

"I appreciate that."

"But if you ever get bored…"

"I know who to call," Cal finished.

Livvie had gone into the kitchen searching for milk,

but she and Tess had apparently found something in common quite quickly. Flynn heard light, feminine laughter drifting from the kitchen, as he and Cal headed in that direction.

"Are you sure you'll be all right tonight?" Cal asked in a lowered voice.

No. "No problem."

"I hate to leave you hanging, but I've already told Livvie that she has to head home first thing in the morning. It's great to have her here, but I don't want her anywhere near this place until we catch Austin."

"I know what you mean," Flynn grumbled, as they reached the kitchen and his eyes were drawn to Tess. Unfortunately, he understood Cal's protective instincts far too well.

"They're sweet," Tess said as she climbed the stairs toward her apartment.

"I'm pretty sure no one's ever called Quinn Calhoun *sweet* before." Flynn was directly behind her, and his steps were heavy and reluctant. "Except maybe Livvie."

Would he remain in the hallway all night? Or come into her room and sleep on the couch? All she knew for certain was that he wouldn't be spending the night in her bed again. Not tonight, not ever.

Knowing that, she should be sorry that she'd made the first move last night, but she wasn't. She was furious with Flynn for leaving in the night, for hiding from her all day, for not caring about her in the way she had come to care about him.

But she wasn't sorry.

At her doorway Flynn faltered, staying in the hallway. Tess turned and faced him, leaning against the doorjamb and looking up into his hard face. If she slammed the door in that face, he would stay in the hallway all night without a word of protest or a single knock on her door. Maybe it was what he deserved. It was certainly what he expected.

She stepped back and opened the door a few inches wider. "Come on in. I'll make you some coffee."

Again, he hesitated.

"I won't bite, and I won't make you *talk,* either."

He stepped inside, and she couldn't tell if he was relieved or not.

While she made coffee, she did talk. Just not about them. There wasn't any *them* to talk about, unless she wanted to torture herself by rehashing everything she'd done wrong.

"Livvie told me she and Cal are going to have a baby. She's so excited. You should have seen her face when she told me the news. I'm surprised she's not already wearing maternity clothes, just so everyone will know."

"Give her a couple of weeks," Flynn said. He sat on the couch, tired and obviously downhearted.

Tess turned, leaning against the counter and watching Flynn while the coffeemaker sputtered. How could she stay mad with the man when he looked like someone had just pulled the rug out from under him? He hadn't seduced her, he hadn't lied about what he wanted from her, he hadn't made promises he wasn't prepared to keep. Should she hold it against him that he wasn't everything she wanted him to be? Had any man she'd ever known lived up to her unrealistic expectations? No. She always expected the men in her life to be perfect. When was she going to learn that no one was perfect? Life was always less than perfection—but oh, she did sometimes long for those rare perfect moments that made such grand memories. Last night had been, in its own way, perfect.

"Errol, huh?" she asked with a smile.

Flynn's head snapped around. "That's not what you and Livvie were laughing about in the kitchen, is it?"

"Of course not. You said that was your deepest secret. Do you think I'm the kind of person who betrays confidences on a whim?"

"No." He leaned back and relaxed, a little.

"That's kind of a silly secret." And she had a feeling that while he didn't want anyone to know his full name, it was far from being his darkest secret.

"It's embarrassing," he said.

"The world is full of John Williams, but there aren't very many Errol Flynns. It's unique, and the world needs variety."

"Yeah, but does the world have to get that variety from me?"

She laughed. A few hours ago she would have thought it impossible to laugh at anything Flynn Benning or any other man said. She liked that—that he could make her laugh.

"Just don't make a big deal out of it," he said. "I don't even know why I told you."

She knew why. Flynn Benning didn't know many ways to give of himself. Sharing a secret was one of them, she imagined. Even something so silly and unimportant as a name. If sharing a secret was his idea of bonding, what would he think if he knew she was keeping a big secret of her own? Not much, she imagined. Good thing they didn't have a relationship to ruin.

"I'm going to take a shower," she said, pushing herself away from the counter. "Coffee will be ready in a couple of minutes, and you know where everything is."

"Yeah. Thanks." Flynn turned on the television and flipped through the three channels she could pick up.

Just before Tess closed the door to her bedroom, she said, "No swashbuckling while I'm gone."

Flynn Benning had to be out of the main building, at least for a few minutes. Just a few minutes.

Tonight the sky was clear and the air was not so cold. Saturday would be a nice day, according to the forecast. All the parents' day outdoor activities would proceed as planned, which would make the job much easier. Rain would drive everyone indoors, and that would make accomplishing the hit more difficult. Not impossible, but still…a nice, clear day that held a touch of spring would be best.

But for tonight, the problem was getting into the main building without running into Benning or any of his men. When it had just been the two women living there, slipping in and out hadn't been much of a problem. Those two kept to their rooms, and there was usually a radio or television playing in the evenings. And if they heard a noise in the night, what were they going to do? Dismiss it as the creaking of an old building, that's what.

But Benning paid more attention than the lunchroom ladies, to those noises that did not belong. Getting caught now, so close to completion, was not an option.

The primary buildings would not do for this particular part of the job. Dr. Barber wouldn't cancel the events planned for Saturday unless she had no other choice; she was much too anal to even consider changing what had become a tradition, and she would do anything, *anything,* to keep from alarming the parents of her precious students.

If one of the buildings that was in use was cordoned off with crime scene tape and detectives were swarming the place, Dr. Barber might not have a choice but to cancel, and the entire plan would have to be reformulated.

This quiet gardener's shed was another matter, however. It could easily be isolated without involving the main area of the campus, and that's what Dr. Barber would do. The nasty business would be handled in a quiet and discreet manner, so as not to disturb the students or the parents.

Worst case, parents' day would be canceled, and the plans would need an adjustment. A *tweaking.* The job would get done, one way or another. It would be worth all the trouble in the world to see Flynn Benning sweat big time.

Serena Loomis and Dante Mangino met here every

night. Not very smart on their part. Routine was dangerous, in this profession. One of them would be along shortly, and the other would follow a few minutes later. In the beginning days they had met on the grounds and walked out here together, but apparently they were being more cautious these days. As if their ploy of leaving their living quarters separately would fool anyone at this point.

It didn't matter which one arrived first; either would do. The math teacher would be easier. She was small and untrained, and the task would be over in a matter of moments. Mangino would be more difficult, but since he'd be taken by surprise the odds would work against him.

Either way, one would be dead, and the other would find the body. Benning would be called, and there would be a window of opportunity in which to slip into the main building.

The door opened, and the beam of a flashlight cut across the darkened shed. A surprised voice asked, "What are you doing here?"

Chapter 10

Flynn listened to the shower run. Tess was in there. Naked. Naked and wet. And she didn't hate him. At least, not entirely. Not yet.

Following her up the stairs tonight, he'd stared at her ass like a kid who'd never seen one up close and personal before. Even that white uniform couldn't take away from the shape and the sway and the curve…. She was one of those rare women who'd look sexy in a gunny sack, and she didn't even know it. He wanted to see her naked one more time, and it just wasn't going to happen.

And she was in there right now, maybe washing her hair….

Flynn was so deeply lost in thought, he almost

jumped when his cell phone rang. Dante's cell number came up on caller ID. Great. Now what?

He answered with a crisp, "Benning."

No response. All was silent. No, not entirely silent. There was breathing on the other end, raspy and uneven.

"Dante?" Flynn leaned forward on the coach, suddenly on alert.

"She's dead." The news was delivered in a voice he hardly recognized as Dante's.

"Who's dead?" Flynn asked as he stood. In the bathroom, the water stopped running.

"Loomis. Serena. He cut her, Major, and she's dead, and I'm going to kill him." The voice was still too soft, but there was a deadly edge to the words Dante spoke.

"Where are you?"

"I walked in, and she was just lying there, and for a minute I didn't know she was dead. It's dark in here."

"Where are you?" Flynn asked again. Loomis's room, Dante's room, the gardener's shed, a storeroom, a deserted teachers' lounge…could be anywhere.

"If I'd left her alone, this never would've happened. If I'd kept my distance there wouldn't have been any reason for him to kill her. He knows, Major. Austin knows we're here, and this is his way of saying hello."

Mangino was very close to snapping, and that couldn't happen. Not tonight.

"Where are you?" Flynn asked one more time, as he headed for Tess's bedroom door.

"Gardener's shed," Dante answered, and then he ended the call.

Flynn knocked loudly on the closed bathroom door. "Tess, I have to leave. I'm going to lock the door behind me. Stay put," he ordered in a voice that left no room for argument. "Don't let anyone into this apartment but me or one of my team, got it?"

"What's wrong?" she asked through the closed door.

"Just promise me you won't let anyone in."

She opened the door. Wrapped in a big white towel, her long red hair wet and curling and her legs peeking out from beneath the towel, she stared up at him. "What happened?"

"I'll tell you later." Right now there was no time, and besides…he didn't know how to break the news. He had never been good at telling people that someone they knew and liked was dead.

But he leaned down and kissed her, quickly but too deep for a woman he had tried all day to put out of his mind. The kiss surprised them both. The fact that he *needed* the kiss shocked the hell out of Flynn. It was everything he had been trying to avoid.

He locked the door to Tess's apartment, and also relocked the entrance to the main building as he left. As he did these things he called Cal and Murphy, in case Dante had not already done so. Neither of them had been notified; his conversations with them were brief, and before he disconnected he ordered Cal to lock his wife in his room with orders not to leave until he got back.

Flynn found Dante in the gardener's shed, sitting on the floor by Serena Loomis's body. Her head was in his lap, and her blood was on the floor, and on the man who held her.

"You shouldn't have moved her," Flynn said in a gentle voice. They weren't detectives, but still...Dante knew better. They all knew better.

"She shouldn't be dead."

"Did you call the locals?"

Dante snorted. "They can't save her, and I'm going to kill Austin myself, so why bother to call the locals?"

Flynn didn't want to know what would happen when a man like Dante Mangino went on a rampage. He had seen a few men snap in his lifetime, and it was never pretty. Someone always got hurt, and it wasn't always the right someone. In a cloud of anger, right and wrong sometimes got hazy.

He knew when Cal and Murphy were standing behind him, even though they hadn't made a sound as they approached. "We have to call someone to take care of her."

"No, that was my job, and I blew it. I blew it big time, Major," Dante said, that scary haze still in his voice. He smoothed her hair way from her face. There was a lot of blood—on the floor, on the dead woman and on Dante.

The local cops were going to immediately home in on Dante as a suspect. He and the victim had been sleeping together; he was a stranger to the area; he had found the body and was covered in her blood—even though he knew better. Eventually they'd be able to explain all that away, but likely not tonight. Not before Saturday, even. Was that the reason for this? Had killing Loomis been a way to distract them from the purpose of this assignment? Or had she seen something she shouldn't have?

"We're not calling the locals," Flynn said as he made his decision, grabbing his cell phone and dialing from memory. "Max can get people in here to take care of the situation."

"Somebody needs to call her father," Dante said, his voice almost calm.

"Not tonight," Flynn said, just before Max Larkin answered the call.

When the phone call was over, Dante lifted his head. "So, we're going to sweep this under the rug? We're going to pretend Serena isn't dead? How the hell can you expect me to do that?"

"I expect you to do whatever has to be done in order to catch the man we came here to catch."

"Catch him, hell," Dante said. "I want him dead."

"Max wants him alive, if possible."

"Max Larkin can kiss my ass. He cut her throat, Major. She didn't fight, she didn't know what was coming, she didn't have a chance to survive. Why should I give Austin a chance?"

"Because it's your job," Flynn said in an insanely calm voice.

What had been a nice late-winter night had turned into a grisly nightmare. Serena Loomis was dead, and the moonlight shining through the open door showed that fact too clearly. Dante was losing it—and Flynn knew too well how he felt. This was their worst nightmare. Innocents weren't supposed to be hurt. The people they loved weren't supposed to be used as diversions or leverage or just for some sick freak's idea of fun.

Cal stepped into the gardener's shed. "Hey, you can do me a favor," he said to Dante. "After this, I don't want Livvie going home alone. You need to get away from here, so why don't you drive her...."

"No," Dante answered in a soft voice. "You drive your wife home, if you think she needs an escort. I'm not going anywhere."

"You really shouldn't—" Cal began.

"Don't push me, Cal. I'm in no mood."

So Cal quit pushing, and the three of them gathered around Serena Loomis's body and the grieving man who held her head on his lap, guarding the woman even though it was too late, protecting Dante as much as they could just by being there.

Flynn had fought so hard and long not to be beholden to anyone or anything. He didn't want a family, he didn't want to care about the people who surrounded him. And crap, here he was with these men he considered family, like it or not. He wanted Cal and Livvie to have a boat-load of babies. They could make their own soccer team, if that's what they wanted. He wanted Murphy to start his own computer company and make a billion bucks. God knows he wasn't cut out for field work. He wanted Dante to forget what had happened here tonight. He wanted the kid's dreams not to be about blood and fu-nerals and empty houses.

He wanted the best for Sadie, too, and for Lucky Santana, who'd likely never had anyone but his women worry about him. Even though all his colleagues were somewhere between five and twelve years younger than he was, in a soul-deep way they felt like his children. The children he had refused to have, after burying Elizabeth and Denise. What a kick in the pants, to realize that he wasn't as free and easy as he'd thought.

It was forty-five minutes before Max's team arrived from Atlanta. Five men arrived on campus without causing a stir and entered the shed quietly. They took Serena Loomis's body away and collected the evidence. And then they cleaned. Not much more than an hour after they'd arrived it was done, and to the casual observer nothing was amiss in the gardener's shed.

Flynn sent Murphy to the men's dorm to check all the surveillance tapes. They didn't have any cameras out this far, but maybe he would see some suspicious movement somewhere on campus. At the moment, that possibility was all they had. Maybe Max's team would come up with something more concrete in the evidence they'd collected—not that they didn't all know who'd murdered Serena Loomis.

It was three in the morning before he returned to Tess's room. She unlocked the door quickly, at his knock. She was rumpled, and there was an equally rumpled pillow and blanket on the couch. She'd been waiting for him.

"You didn't ask who was at the door," he grumbled.

"I recognized your knock, and your footstep in the hallway. I knew it was you, so save the third degree. What happened?"

He just stared down at her. How could he tell her what he'd found in the gardener's shed, and how they'd covered it up? How could he let that part of his life touch hers?

She took his hand and drew him into the apartment, closing and locking the door behind him. "Is there a problem with the students?"

Flynn shook his head.

"Is it…" she began, and then she stopped. "Never mind," she said in a gentled voice. "We'll worry about this later. You look like you could use some sleep."

Sleep? He didn't know if he'd ever sleep again. Loomis was dead. Murphy was scanning the night's tapes and babysitting a broken Dante, and Cal was driving Livvie back to Alabama, where he would leave her with an armed guard until this was all over. Just in case.

Flynn touched Tess's cheek, caressed the soft skin with his thumb. She was so pretty and so temptingly sexy—even in those silky pajamas with the pink bunnies and her fuzzy slippers. She was special, like it or not. Somehow he was going to have to let her know that he hadn't thought of last night as a mistake, without promising her more than he had to give.

"I have never been so glad to see anyone as I am to see you now," he said honestly.

The expression on Flynn's face scared her. There was a darkness in his eyes that spoke of secrets well beyond something so meaningless as an embarrassing name.

"You said that men like me think we can fix everything."

"I guess I did," she whispered.

His finger kept working across her cheek. "You were right. My worst nightmare is coming face-to-face with something I can't fix."

"You can't expect to make everything that's wrong right," she said.

"I can, actually," he said. "Those things that are given to me to make right, anyway. But every now and then, just when I think I have everything under control…it all falls apart on me, and I realize what a joke it is that I think I can control anything."

Her arms slipped around his waist, and she held on tight. She pressed her ear to his chest, closed her eyes and listened to his heartbeat. "Is that why you think you can't get involved with me?"

"Yeah." His fingers raked through her hair.

"That's not a good enough reason."

"I thought maybe it was," he said softly. "Now I'm not so sure. Right now I'm not sure of much of anything."

She ran her hands up and down his back, in an automatic gesture of comfort. Flynn seemed to need the comfort, and she wanted to touch him. A hundred questions were racing through her mind, but for a moment she just held on, listened to him breathe, and offered solace and warmth.

But after a few minutes, she pulled away from him and looked into his face, again. "What happened?"

His face remained hard, but she saw the vulnerability there, the pain he tried to hide. Did he carry the things he couldn't fix with him eternally?

"Serena Loomis is dead," he said. "The man we came here to catch...odds are he killed her."

Tess's heart skipped a beat and her knees wobbled, and as if he knew she was suddenly unsteady, Flynn's hold on her tightened.

"Nobody knows but us, not yet."

"You have to call the sheriff, Flynn, you can't just—"

"Federal investigators are handling the case, and her body. The investigation will be ten times better than anything we could dream of seeing from the local sheriff's department. We'll get him, I promise you that."

"How's Mangino?" she whispered.

"How the hell do you think he is?" Flynn answered gruffly.

A cold shiver worked through her body. She could imagine, too well, what it must be like to discover that someone you thought was going to be here tomorrow wasn't going to be here ever again.

One large hand cupped the back of her neck, and Flynn held on. "I kept thinking, while I watched Dante fall apart...that could've been you, lying on the floor in a puddle of blood. Austin could've decided to kill you in order to send us a message. He chose Loomis because she was easier. She was *there*. But it could've been you, and if you want to know why I can't afford to get involved with you or any other woman, there it is. You think you can protect the people you care about, but you can't. Not all the time. Not every day."

"Are we talking about me now, or Serena Loomis, or your wife?"

"What difference does it make?" he asked.

"It makes a lot of difference to me."

Flynn pulled her close so she couldn't see his face. "Loomis is dead and Dante is caught up in a grief so deep he can't see daylight, and all I can think about is that it wasn't you. I'm glad it wasn't you, Red. I don't think I could survive if it was you."

He revealed more than he'd intended, with those words. That and the way he held her proved that he cared more than he knew. Maybe he could love her. Maybe he already loved her, a little.

"It wasn't me," she whispered. "I'm right here, and I'm not going anywhere."

"I know that." He was already recovering, a little, setting tonight's shock and pain somewhere deep inside, where it wouldn't hurt so much. But it wasn't gone. It would never be entirely gone. She knew that. Regret had a way of living on, no matter what you did to relieve it.

She reached up and raked a thumb across a stubbly jaw. "Come to bed with me, and hold me for a while, and sleep."

"I won't sleep tonight," he said.

"Then don't," she responded. "All I ask is that if you decide you have to leave while I'm asleep, you'll wake me and tell me that you're going. I don't want to wake up surprised to find myself alone. That's no fun."

"I'm sorry."

"Don't tell me you're sorry, Flynn. Just…do things differently this time."

He kissed her, more desperate than ever before. There

was heart and desperation and passion in that kiss. Pain, too, asking to be released and relieved.

"I need you, Red," he said as they began to walk toward the bedroom.

"I need you, too."

They didn't rush, but before they'd reached the doorway her pajama top was unbuttoned. She wasn't sure how he'd managed that so quickly and easily, but he had. The top fell open, and cool air hit her bare skin. And then Flynn's hands were there, caressing and warming.

She wanted to feel his skin against hers, that was all. Warm arms, hard flesh, strong heartbeat.

She unbuttoned his shirt and pushed it off his shoulders, and ran her hands down his arms, slowly. He was so strong, in so many ways. But he was also human, and he did need her. When she reached for his pants, he stopped her.

"I don't have another condom," he said gently.

She sighed, and her heartbeat slowed a little. "I thought you were one of those guys who's always prepared."

"I wasn't prepared for you, Red. In so many ways, I was not prepared for you."

"I think I'll take that as a compliment."

"You should." He cupped one breast and teased the nipple with one thumb. "Don't you have some old… anything, hidden away somewhere?"

She laughed. "No. I haven't needed any *anything* in a few years, so…"

"Years?" he asked. "Before last night it was…"

"Years," she said as she reached up to touch his face

again. The way they touched slowed, but it was no less passionate. It was different than before, but just as intimate. Perhaps more so. "I understand there are a lot of women out there who are discriminating enough to go years without sex, if the right man doesn't come along. There's no reason to look at me like I just sprouted a second head."

But he did. He studied her in a way that made her squirm. "Why me?" he finally asked.

"Don't ask me that question when you're not prepared to hear the answer."

She expected him to walk away, to leave her and the room and take up residence on the couch again, or maybe in the hallway. But he didn't leave. She drew back the covers and crawled into bed, after kicking off her slippers. Flynn stripped down to his boxers and crawled into bed with her. He drew her into his embrace and went very still.

Tess wanted to make him forget what he'd seen tonight, at least for a while. Not with sex. She was fairly sure there would be time for that another night. She wasn't a hundred percent sure, but then what was truly certain in this world? Not much, if anything.

She snuggled against him, her face resting against his chest. She hadn't bothered to grab her pajama top before crawling into the bed, so her bare torso was pressed to his. She liked it, very much.

"You can talk, if you want," she whispered.

"Just go to sleep," Flynn replied, his voice gruff and faint.

"I can't sleep. Not yet, at least."

There was a full moon tonight, and it cast light through the window to illuminate her room and the bed they laid upon. Flynn was so long and big he made her bed look and feel full. Complete. Right. What would she do when he was gone, and her nights became solitary once again?

"It's not your fault, you know," she said.

"Feels like it."

"You can't live like that, Flynn, taking on every tragedy as your own. You'll catch the man who did this, I know you will. There's nothing else you can do."

His hand moved up and down her bare back, gently. She wasn't sure if he was offering comfort or taking it, and it didn't really matter. "Today, when I was actually teaching history class and actually freakin' liking it, I allowed myself to believe that the tip that brought us here was bogus. In my mind Austin was a thousand miles away, and everyone here was safe, and there was a logical explanation for everything that seemed suspicious up until this point. I let my guard down, Red. I let myself believe that I lived in another world. And now Loomis is dead."

"Allowing yourself a moment of peace doesn't mean the world is going to fall apart. You're entitled to peace, Flynn. Everyone has that right." And maybe if he realized that he was allowed to be happy, he wouldn't be so quick to write off what they had...or might have, if things went their way. "Maybe I give you a hard time, now and then, but the world needs men who want to fix things. The world needs men like you."

Tess knew she needed a man like Flynn, at least for a while. She needed him here, and in the kitchen, and sitting on her couch, and drinking her coffee, and making her feel like she was important with a smile or a laugh or a word. If she confessed as much, if she said *I need a man like you,* would he run again? She wasn't going to take that chance.

"It's not your fault," she whispered.

"You never did explain to me, in a way that makes any sense, why you're here," he said, blatantly changing the subject. "Your last job paid twice what you're making here, and…"

"Don't turn the tables on me just because you don't like the way the conversation is going." She wouldn't lie to him, not tonight, but it wasn't time for that conversation. The way things were going, it might not ever be time. "Right now, it doesn't matter why I'm here, and I'm not even going to ask how you know how much I made at my last job."

"I have my ways," he said softly.

"I don't doubt it."

They lay there, snuggled close and wide-awake, hearts pounding in the night, hands touching but not exploring. Not tonight. After a while, sleep began to creep in, slowly but surely. Tess's heartbeat slowed, her eyes drifted shut.

"I'm glad you're here, Red," Flynn said, threading his fingers through her hair and holding on tight. "You're a pain in the ass, and I worry about you, and I know I've already screwed up any chance we have of…anything. But I'm still glad you're here."

"You haven't completely screwed up," she whispered. "Good."

Finally they both slept, half-naked and entwined. Right before she drifted off, Tess wondered if she would wake up to find Flynn almost inside her and then joined with her so quickly and perfectly, like last night, but of course that was a chance he wouldn't take. A man who was vehemently opposed to fathering a child wasn't going to take that risk. Sometime toward dawn she woke just long enough to realize that Flynn was awake and that he held her, still.

When next she woke he was dressed and hovering above her. He stroked her cheek as he woke her, saying, "Get dressed, Red. You're leaving."

Chapter 11

The girls were confused and Dr. Barber was having a conniption fit in the parking lot, where two long buses sat with their engines running.

"I don't think this is wise," the headmistress said as she watched the students file onto the waiting buses for an unannounced field trip.

Flynn glared down at her. The woman was no more than five foot two, and she was pushing retirement hard and fast, but she wasn't easily intimidated. Reminded him of a sergeant he had once…. "One of your teachers was murdered last night," he said in a lowered voice, so that none of the girls would hear. "Her throat was cut, and she bled out on the floor of the gardener's shed." Maybe a dose of reality would shake some sense into the old woman. Judging by the way she paled, maybe the plan worked. "I don't know about you, but I'd feel better if these kids were somewhere else while we look for the killer."

"And if you don't find the killer?" she snapped with authority.

"We'll find him."

Dr. Barber wrung her hands in uncharacteristic indecision. "The parents will be arriving in the morning. If you haven't done your job by then, what will I tell them about what's happened? How will I explain?"

"Tell them their children are being protected by their teachers and federal marshals," Flynn snapped. The buses would be met in Atlanta, and after that the students and teachers would be in the custody of the government until this was settled, thanks to Max Larkin. With any luck, the girls would never know they were being protected.

Out of the corner of his eye, Flynn saw Tess speaking with Laura Stokes and Bev Martin, calmly explaining what was going on, as best she could. He excused himself to walk to the threesome, leaving a distraught Dr. Barber pacing and wringing her hands.

Tess wasn't wearing her usual kitchen garb today. Instead she wore a pair of faded jeans, leather boots and a green sweater that molded to her very nice form. Her hair was loose, and it curled over her shoulders and down her back. God, he wished he was somewhere else, with her. On the beach, in a mountain cabin, upstairs in her bed. He wanted to thread his fingers through her hair and slip his hand beneath that sweater and start all over. He wanted to start everything all over again.

Last night he'd just held Tess, and somehow it had been more intimate than the sex. It was scary stuff, to let himself get that close to a woman again. It had been a long time, and he wasn't sure he was ready to get that deeply involved with a woman...or would ever be ready. His life now was relatively neat, the occasional tragedy like Serena Loomis's death aside. Getting involved with Tess was only going to mess that neatness up, big time.

As he approached, Tess turned to look at him. Laura and Bev did the same. If it was a time for smiling, maybe he would've done just that. But there really wasn't anything to smile about. Not personally, not professionally. All three women had questions in their eyes, questions he couldn't answer. At least, not yet.

The way the morning sunlight hit those three faces apparently caused a trick of the light, because for a moment, just a moment, in the haze of the morning sun, Tess and Laura looked so much alike they could be twins. Tess's hair was darker and not so curly, and Laura hadn't yet grown into herself, but there was a definite similarity in the shape of their faces and the cant of their shoulders and even the way they stood. They both had long legs and a slight upturn to their noses. The shape of their mouths was almost identical.

Flynn blinked hard. No, not twins. Mother and daughter.

No wonder Tess was here. This explained everything—why she was working in the cafeteria, why she'd refused to leave the campus, why she was so protective of all the girls, like any mother would be.

"What's going on, Mr. Benning?" Laura asked. "There was nothing about a field trip on the schedule."

Flynn kept his cool, and for Laura and Bev he did manage to smile. A little. They didn't know about Loomis's murder, or that a killer named Austin was nearby, or the fact that their substitute history teacher was armed and definitely dangerous.

"The opportunity for an exclusive tour of a series of government buildings in Atlanta came up at the last minute. It was too good to pass up."

"Tomorrow is parents' day, and we have a soccer game in the afternoon," Laura insisted.

"You'll be back here in plenty of time for all that." *Maybe.* "I'm going to ask Tess here to take special care of my favorite students. Y'all are going to have a great time."

Laura glanced back at the bus. "These are just the live-in students. Aren't we going to wait for the girls from town?"

"No. This is a special treat just for the students who are living here." Early morning phone calls were keeping the girls from town at home.

"A day off is a special treat," Laura argued.

"Quit arguing with me and scoot," Flynn said in a slightly gruff voice, knowing Laura could very well argue with him all morning.

"You're not going?" Bev asked, her voice much too soft, as always.

"I wish I could, but someone's got to hold down the fort." He directed them to the second bus, and reluctantly they went. Tess started to follow, but he grabbed her arm and she fell back against him, soft and easy.

She looked up at him, afraid and uncertain about this whole idea. But she did trust him. Not enough, apparently, but some.

"You could've told me," he said, his voice so low no one else would hear.

"Told you what?" she asked, almost innocently. Behind her, Laura and Bev were getting onto the second bus, along with a grumbling Melody Matthews and a confused Stephanie McCabe.

"No bull, Tess," he said. "We're past that, I hope. No, I know without doubt that we're past that. At least now I understand why you're here, when you could be anywhere else in the world."

He saw the panic in her eyes. Was she afraid that he wouldn't understand why she'd kept the truth from him? Or was her fear that he'd tell her secret? He leaned down and kissed her on the cheek, and whispered close to her ear. "She's just like you, Red. Relentless and pretty and aggravating as hell. Does she know?"

Tess gripped his arm and answered, her voice just as soft. "No."

"Are you going to tell her?"

"I haven't decided."

He nodded. She'd told him enough of the story for him to piece the rest together. Most of it, anyway.

"You're not mad?" she asked.

"At you? No way, Red."

She sighed, obviously relieved. "Be careful. You and I have a lot to talk about when we get back."

"Scary words. I'm not all that good at talking."

"You're much better than you think you are."

She kissed him, not on the cheek but square on the lips. Apparently she wasn't worried about the fact that others were watching, from a distance. He kissed her back, because it felt right and because he could. When the kiss ended, much too soon, she smiled up at him, gently.

"Go get 'im, swashbuckler."

Tess took the seat behind Laura and Bev, relieved that she would be able to keep an eye on them while the bus headed for Atlanta. Why was it that buses always smelled so nasty? She wrinkled her nose as she checked out the other passengers.

Stephanie McCabe was giving skin care tips to a poor girl who had the misfortune to be sitting beside the English teacher. Leon Toller sat near the back of the bus, and as usual he was muttering to himself. A couple of teachers from the high school sat together, and from the way they were whispering they were obviously wondering what was going on. The students talked and laughed and some even sang. Melody Matthews seemed to be falling asleep.

They didn't know yet that their math teacher had been murdered. When they were told, the mood would change. Kids shouldn't be confronted with violence, not in any way, but sometimes the unthinkable happened.

The students were a little bewildered by the unannounced field trip, but like all kids they'd adjusted quickly. Life was an adventure, and if it threw you a curve ball you might as well catch it.

Flynn was definitely a curve ball. Tess's life had to be dedicated to working out this situation with Laura. There wasn't time for a man. And yet, here he was. There was no denying that in a short period of time he had become important to her.

They were less than thirty minutes down the road when Melody Matthews woke, stretched her arms over her head and slipped across the aisle to take the seat beside Tess.

"I didn't expect this," the surly teenager said.

"None of us did." Tess tried a smile she didn't feel. The way the sunlight shone on the girl's face and her hair…it almost looked like there were pale blond roots beneath very plain brown strands of hair. Had to be the light. Why would a blonde dye her hair such an ordinary brown?

"We'll make the best of it," Tess said with a false brightness.

"I'm going to try," Melody said. "What other choice do I have?"

"That's a good attitude."

"I'm glad you think so." Tess felt the press of the muzzle in her side before she looked down and saw the gun. "Daddy always says I have a good attitude about the little problems that come our way."

* * *

While the men who'd been left behind to guard the campus headed toward the dormitory where they'd set up their base of operations, Dale sneaked into the main building and up the stairs, to the storeroom. He'd retrieve his weapon, and wait. He'd overheard one of them mention running the tapes from last night again. That should take some time.

He really should consider working solo, for a while. His partner was, at times, completely unreasonable. It wasn't that murder hadn't crossed his mind a time or two, but a fire in an outbuilding would've gotten Benning out of this building just as well as murder. Had his "daughter" listened to him? No.

Last night's plan had backfired. The kids were gone, and Benning and his men were going to tear the campus to pieces until they found what they were looking for. Parents' day would be canceled. Months of planning and waiting for the right opportunity, wasted.

He'd slipped into the men's dormitory and this main building several times, over the past four months, looking through the Martin kid's records and scouting out the perfect place to set up for the execution. Only twice had he left behind evidence of his presence. The headmistress should have discounted the break-ins as childish mischief—but she hadn't. What surprised Dale most was that anyone besides Barber had taken the incidents seriously. It shouldn't have happened. Benning shouldn't be here.

Flynn Benning and his team had made it necessary

that the plans be altered, but that didn't mean the job would be canceled. Wyatt Martin was damned impossible to get close to during his day-to-day business operations. The man traveled frequently and his hours were erratic, which made planning ahead difficult, if not impossible. But he did dote on his only child, and they had always known that sooner or later Martin would be here at the Frances Teague Academy, where the security was lax and his guard would be down.

Martin didn't have any idea his business partner wanted him out of the way, which made things all the easier.

Parents' day would have offered the perfect opportunity for a quick execution. Melody would lead the target into the open, and Dale would make the shot. By the time anyone figured out where the shot had come from, he'd be well away from here. That opportunity was gone, but still, Martin would likely offer himself up in exchange for his only daughter. One way or another the job would get done.

By now, Melody should've taken control of the bus. Dale glanced at his watch. If not, then in just a few more minutes. It was distressing that it had become necessary to involve the children, but that was Benning's fault. If he'd kept his nose out of their business, then none of this would've been necessary. The math teacher would still be alive, and the kids wouldn't have to suffer a nasty scare, and in twenty-six hours or so Wyatt Martin would be dead. That part of the scenario hadn't changed, even though the method had been altered.

Dale recovered his rifle from its hiding place. Benning and the others had made this job much more difficult than it should've been, and he was going to make them pay. From the window from which he had planned to shoot Wyatt Martin, he would pick off the party-crashers one at a time. It was only fitting.

He grabbed his ammunition from yet another hiding place, sat on the floor with his back against the wall, and began to load. He was sitting there when the door to the storeroom was kicked open.

Benning, with the other three right behind him, stormed into the room. Their pistols were drawn, and they were not surprised to see him. The rifle popped up and he took aim at Benning's midsection. "Close enough."

None of them so much as slowed down. "That rifle won't work too well without the firing pin."

"You're bluffing." Dale cocked the weapon and fired, but nothing happened.

And four large, fully loaded pistols were pointed at his head. Dale dropped the rifle and raised his hands. They could have him, for now. He knew they wouldn't dare kill him. He had information which was much more valuable to them than their own macho revenge.

He also had a *very* good lawyer he hadn't yet needed to call on.

Dante Mangino worked his way around Benning. There was a small flaw in the plan. That one very well might kill him. The long-haired tough took aim, narrowing one dark eye.

"I didn't kill her," Dale said quickly.

"Right," Mangino said softly as the gun moved closer.

"Not yet," Benning instructed calmly.

"Why not?" Mangino asked, his eyes eerily calm.

"Don't you want to know who did kill your girl-friend?" Dale asked.

His answer was a kick to the cheek, a solid blow that snapped his head around and drew blood and made him feel as if his head had been loosened from his shoulders.

Dale wiped the blood from his mouth and looked up at Benning. "Get him away from me, or your little play-mate is next. Do you really think I've been working alone all this time? Do you really think I don't have all my bases covered?"

Benning ordered Mangino to back off, and he did. But not much.

"My partner is on the bus. She's in complete control. Maybe you and I can come to some sort of agreement that will see everyone through today alive and well. What do you say to a trade, Benning?"

No one said a word. Of course, once again Dale had the upper hand. What choice did they have?

A partner. Crap. All that uncertainty about whether or not Austin was male or female…Austin was both. They were a team.

Flynn had found and disabled the rifle early this morning, before he'd gone to Tess and told her what had happened to Serena Loomis. That was when he'd de-

cided to get them all out of harm's way. A couple of
phone calls later, and the arrangements had been made.

"Your partner, who is she?" Flynn asked.

The middle-aged man on the floor looked entirely too
smug. "For the past seven years she has been my daughter, my wife, my sister, even my brother. She's quite
good with disguises, actually."

"Dante, kick him again."

"Wait, I'll tell you what you…" Before Austin could
say more, Dante had done as he was told.

When he'd recovered from the kick, Austin lifted
his head. "I told you, I didn't kill her. I don't care
much for the knife—it's too messy and close for my
taste."

"Austin, Texas, five years ago." Flynn said.

"I was there, but I didn't kill the man in question."

"Your partner?"

Austin nodded. "She actually prefers to work up
close, if you get my drift."

A woman who liked the knife was with Tess. A knot
formed in Flynn's stomach, and it wasn't going away
until he knew everyone on that bus was safe. And if they
weren't…

"Give me a name."

"It's too late for that," Austin said, and then he looked
up at Dante, waiting for another kick that didn't come.
"If you contact anyone on the bus she'll just panic and
start killing people. She has a bit of a hair trigger. Might
as well let things play out."

"A trade, huh?"

Austin tried to smile, but his face was damaged and the effort was a poor one. "A trade."

"Is the driver armed?" Melody asked in a lowered voice.

"I don't know." Tess's heart beat so fast she could feel it, pounding away. "I don't think so."

Melody leaned slightly into the aisle and sniffled in disgust. "Unlikely, though I have seen more than a few over-the-hill potbellied cops in my day. Might be best if we just get rid of him. Can you drive this thing?"

"Don't do anything rash," Tess hissed.

"I never do anything *rash*." Melody's eyes scanned the crowded bus. No one else seemed to realize what was happening. "We're going back toward the school." She jabbed gently with the weapon. "There's a small park between Thorndale and the campus. Do you know it?"

"Yes."

"Get the driver to take us there, or I'm going to start shooting people. You don't want that, do you?"

"No," Tess whispered. "I don't want that." In the seat just ahead, Laura and Bev were whispering to one another, giggling the way girls do with their best friends. "I have a better idea. How about we put the driver and the students off, and you and I go back to the park in the bus?" she suggested. "I'm sure I can figure out how to drive it."

Melody shook her head. "That won't do. I need the girls."

Tess tried to reason with Melody. "If any of the girls

get hurt, there's no turning back. You don't want to mess up your life this way," she said calmly. "You're so young, you have your whole life ahead of you." She thought about what little Flynn had told her about the man they were looking for. He'd suspected that perhaps someone from the school was helping the man they were hunting. He'd never suspected a student. "An impressionable girl your age, I can understand how you might get involved with a man who promises you the moon. But it won't be as easy as you think, to kill someone, to take a life. I don't know what you think you're going to accomplish by…"

The girl's wicked smile silenced Tess. "I'm not all that much younger than you are," she said. "A few years, maybe. It's the hairstyle and the makeup and the clothes that make me look young. Maybe I have good genes to account for the fact that I can still pass for seventeen. Since I never knew my parents, I can't say if that's the case or not."

"You said your father…"

"The Daddy bit?" Melody grinned. "Dale is the only family I've ever known, but he's not my father. For this job, he's Daddy. He put on quite a show for Dr. Barber, telling the old bat what a troublemaker I'd been at all those other schools. He's been around a lot, lately, but no one ever saw him. No one but me."

"But surely there's a way…"

Melody leaned in very close and whispered in Tess's ear. "I killed Ms. Loomis so quick she didn't even have a chance to make a sound. She was just surprised, and then she died. Stall for another minute, and I'll just pick the closest kid to be the next victim."

The closest kid was Laura.

Dante wanted to kill Austin, and in a way he had not expected, so did Flynn. But for now, he didn't have a lot of choice in the matter.

Flynn's cell phone rang, and he snagged it as Cal and Murphy dragged Austin to his feet.

"Benning."

"We've lost the other bus." Dr. Barber's husky voice was unmistakable.

The headmistress and most of the older girls were on the first bus. Her words only confirmed what Austin had said. "They've already called me," Flynn said, his eyes on Austin's face. "Engine trouble."

"We'll turn back…" Dr. Barber began.

"No. Don't. Someone's already on their way to check it out. You just go on. They'll meet you in Atlanta, as planned."

Dr. Barber didn't like the idea of being separated from half of her students, but eventually she agreed and ended the phone call.

"The next phone call should be for me," Austin said, more calm than he should've been, given the situation. Did he really think he was going to walk away from this?

Sure enough, Austin's cell phone rang. Cal retrieved the phone, flipped it open, and held it to the wounded man's ear. Flynn stood close enough to listen to both sides of the conversation.

Austin didn't bother with greetings. Instead he answered with, "We have a bit of a problem."

"What kind of a problem?" Melody asked sharply.

The bus was headed back toward the school—or rather, that park near campus. Melody held her gun to the bus driver's head, and the girls were all silent and afraid. Even the teachers had gone quiet. No amount of makeup was going to disguise the fact that Stephanie McCabe had gone colorless with fear.

Tess stood directly behind Melody, trying to be a buffer between the kids and the woman who had taken the bus. Once they were off the bus, she'd separate the girls from Melody and wrestle with her long enough to give the kids a chance to escape.

She was more than willing to risk getting shot if it meant Laura and the other girls would get out of this situation.

"Trade?" Melody asked sharply. "Are you kidding me?"

After listening for a few more minutes, she said, "Fine," and ended the call with a fierce flick of her thumb. She leaned over and spoke to the driver. "Forget the park. We're going back to the school."

He nodded, and then Melody looked at Tess. How could she have passed for a student, all these months? Sure, she looked young enough, but there was no innocence in her dark eyes. Only pain and anger and determination. How had she hidden that malice so well?

"I go back to high school—which I dearly hated the

first time around—play dumb for months, kill the math teacher, take a busful of kids hostage…and what am I going to get out of it? My partner in one piece, if all goes well. The job is shot, for now, which means we won't get paid on schedule. We have to start over, with a new plan. And if Benning figures out who the target is and warns him, he'll increase security and go underground and it'll be next to impossible to get to him. Months of work, all for nothing."

"If everyone gets out of this alive, it's not all for nothing," Tess said, trying to remain calm and to project some of that calm onto Melody.

"I'm not so sure everyone's getting out of this alive," Melody said, as she turned her eyes to the road ahead. "In fact, I'd have to say it's damned unlikely."

Chapter 12

The bus pulled into the parking lot. After it came to a stop and the engine was shut down, the automatic door opened with a whoosh. One by one, the kids rushed off. They were terrified; shaking and pale and doing their best to huddle together. Flynn motioned them to the side, where Murphy was waiting to lead them into the closest building—the main hall where the cafeteria and the headmistress's office and Tess's apartment were all located.

Flynn held his breath, waiting for Tess to walk down the bus steps. She likely wouldn't get off until all the kids were safe, so he didn't expect her to step down at the front of the line. But still, waiting was tougher than it should've been.

Most of the kids were off the bus, and so were a couple of the teachers, but he still hadn't seen Laura or Bev. Maybe he'd lost them in the crowd, but that was unlikely. Stephanie McCabe exited, along with the only other teacher remaining on the bus, a fumbling, frightened Leon Toller. McCabe glanced back into the bus, and her step stuttered a little, as if she were uncertain about walking away.

Flynn did more than hold his breath, in the moments after McCabe was guided into the main building. No one else got off the bus, after the English teacher.

A shrill voice called from the bus. "I want to see him!"

Flynn nodded, and Cal dragged a swollen and bleeding Austin into the open.

Again, Melody's voice was shrill. "Maybe I should send out one of these girls looking like that."

Flynn tried to peer into the bus, but he couldn't see much. The driver, a gun in a woman's hand, one blue-jeaned leg. Tess's, if he wasn't mistaken. Just the sight of that leg calmed him, somewhat. "He's fair game," Flynn called out, "and so am I. So are you. They're not, and you know it. Let's get this over with."

"The car's ready?"

"Yeah."

A getaway vehicle—the one Austin had directed them to—was parked close by with the keys in the ignition, a tank full of gas…and a tracking device attached to the back bumper.

The driver exited the bus first, meaty hands in the air. Melody was next. She held a gun to the driver's head, and used his large body as a shield. Beside and slightly behind her, Bev Martin was all but dragged down the steps. Melody had a tight grip on the girl's wrist. Tess and Laura brought up the rear, clinging to one another in fear, but neither of them panicking.

When he saw them, alive and unhurt, Flynn could finally breathe right again.

"This is what's going to happen," Melody called, barely peeking over the bus driver's shoulder. "You send my partner over, and I'll let a couple of these hostages go."

"You let 'em all go," Flynn responded.

"Do you think I'm stupid? The bus driver and the kid are coming with us, until we're sure you're not going to try anything sneaky."

"No kids," Flynn said. "That's not negotiable."

"Everything is negotiable, Benning."

He signaled Cal to release Austin, and the wounded man stumbled toward his partner. When he was almost there, Melody said something to Tess, in a lowered voice. Tess took Laura's arm and tried to lead her away from the bus...but Laura fought.

"I'm not leaving Bev with *her*." Laura planted her feet as Tess tried to drag her away from danger.

"You want to come along?" Melody snapped. "We can always make room for one more."

Tess looked desperate, and so did Laura. Tess was frantic to protect her child, and the kid was determined not to leave her friend behind, which was admirable and brave and incredibly stupid. Was he the only one who saw how much she was like her mother?

Flynn holstered his weapon, lifted his hands to show Melody that he wasn't armed, and took long, quick steps toward the redheads. When he reached them he lifted Laura off her feet and carried her toward Murphy. She fought for a while, kicking and yelling at him to put her down, until he said in a lowered voice, "Trust me, kid." Then she went still. The noise that escaped from her throat was one of sheer terror. Not for herself, but for her friend.

When he placed Laura on her on her feet, Tess took charge of the girl and together they ran into the main building. When they were out of sight, safe behind brick walls, Flynn was able to take a deep breath and concentrate on the problem at hand.

The bus driver, Austin, Melody and Bev were on one side of the parking lot, and Flynn and his three men spread across the other. If not for Bev, this could be over very quickly.

"Don't take the kid," Flynn said. "If you want a hostage in addition to the bus driver, take me."

"Like anyone's going to care if we rough *you* up," Melody answered cynically. She and the man they'd always called Austin, along with their two hostages, began to edge toward the getaway car. With the tracking device they could keep up with where the car was headed, but anything could happen once they were out of sight. They could have another car waiting a short way down the road. In fact, they'd be stupid not to. No way could he allow Austin and his partner to get in that car with Bev.

"Taking me's forgivable," Flynn argued. "Kidnap-

ping her isn't. The whole world is going to come down
on you if you hurt that kid."

"Let it come down," Melody replied.

The bus driver stumbled, falling to his knees, and in
response Melody yanked Bev in front of her, to replace
the shield she'd lost. She didn't notice the bus driver
reaching for his ankle, as he tried clumsily to stand.
Austin was more concerned with the injuries to his face
than anything else, so he only spared the driver a disgusted glance. As far as he was concerned, his partner
had everything under control…as under control as a situation like this one could be.

Cal focused his attention on Bev, shouting sharply,
"From behind, number three," and then several things
happened at once.

The normally quiet Bev screamed at the top of her
lungs, surprising Melody as she twisted sharply to escape
her kidnapper's grip, using her body weight and her el-
bows as Cal had taught her. Then she dropped, rolled and
jumped up to run away from the immediate danger, taking shelter around the front side of the bus. The driver came
up holding a small pistol that had been concealed in an
ankle holster, and he rolled onto his back to fire up at a surprised Melody. And as Austin realized what was happening and went for the gun Melody had dropped, Flynn fired.

With the sounds of gunfire still reverberating in the
air, Cal and Murphy closed in on the wounded assassins. Flynn holstered his gun and ran toward Bev. She
saw him, and ran. Toward him, not away. When she
was just a few feet from him, she started to cry.

Flynn lifted Bev off her feet and carried her toward the main building, while she gripped his neck and sobbed. Her tears fell against his neck and dampened his shirt, and her hold on him was fierce. Bullets were easier than tears. He'd done everything he knew to do, and still he felt helpless.

"Don't cry. It's okay now," he said, anxious to get the kid to Tess so he could handle more important matters…like getting Max's men in here and seeing if either of the assassins were going to make it. He didn't need to ask who the target of the planned assassination had been. Bev hadn't been chosen at random to be their hostage. "The bad guys are down, and no one else is hurt. That's all that matters."

Dante had backed up a ways, and stood between the excitement and the building where the students had taken cover. Flynn knew why he wasn't with Cal and Murphy and the federal marshal who had been posing as a bus driver. If he got too close to the woman who'd killed Serena Loomis, he wouldn't be able to control himself.

Flynn knew that if Tess hadn't gotten off that bus he would have felt the same way. As it was, Max wanted at least one of them alive, and that was still possible. They'd want to know who'd hired Austin and his partner.

Tess met him at the door and took custody of a still-sobbing Bev. Laura was right behind her mother…the woman she had no idea was her mother…and together they comforted the girl who'd been personally threatened by the cold-blooded killer they'd believed to be a student.

Tess lifted her head and her eyes met his. "Is any-one hurt?"

"Just the bad guys."

She closed her eyes and nodded, in obvious relief.

"The bus driver had a gun," Bev said, recovering slowly from her panic.

"Of course he did," Flynn said. "Do you think I'd put you on that bus without an armed guard?"

"No," Tess answered softly.

He leaned down and kissed her, quick. "Feed the girls, talk to them, tell them everything is okay. But don't let them out of the building until I tell you the parking lot's been cleared." They didn't need to see even the worst among them wounded.

"You got it," she said.

Flynn looked at Laura and Bev. Laura was comfort-ing her friend, and they both looked at him for expla-nation he couldn't give them. Tess had them now, and his job was done. It wasn't necessary for him to say an-other word. So why was he so sure handling the details in the parking lot weren't so freakin' important, after all?

"You girls going to be okay?" he asked.

Bev, who had stopped sobbing but was still badly shaken, nodded and said, "Da-da-damn skippy."

Tess sat in her apartment, sipping decaf. It had been such a long day, maybe the longest of her life, and she still shook, now and then.

Several of the parents had come to the school to col-lect their children, after learning what had happened this morning. Bev's father had been one of them, but Laura was still on campus. Jack would be here tomorrow, as planned, and after that…who knew? He might leave Laura here, he might not. If Jack took Laura away, what would she do?

Another group of men—more of *those guys*—had descended on the campus for several hours after the shooting. Tess had spoken to more than one of them, telling her story of what had happened on the bus again and again, until they were satisfied. They had been surprisingly gentle with the girls they interviewed, in a way she knew Flynn would have been if it had been his job. He had more gentleness inside him than he would ever admit. She'd seen that tenderness, more than once.

It was over. The man—and woman—Flynn had come here to catch were no longer a danger to anyone at the Frances Teague Academy, or anywhere else. Both of them were wounded, and if they survived they'd be locked away, as was right and proper.

Even though the danger was past, Tess still felt restless and uneasy. She'd tried to get her daughter to spend the night here in the apartment above the kitchen, with her, but Laura had been reluctant to leave her own room in the girls' dorm. Tess hadn't pushed the matter. After all, Laura didn't know Tess was her mother. A group of the older girls had taken it upon themselves to sit with the students who had been on the hijacked bus and hadn't yet been retrieved by their parents, so they wouldn't have to be alone tonight. That was the only thing that kept Tess from camping outside her daughter's door, the way Flynn had once camped outside hers.

Tess placed her coffee cup on the kitchen counter. It was late. She really should just go to bed and try to get some sleep, but at the moment she didn't feel like she'd ever sleep again.

She heard his step in the hallway, and that soft sound was met with a rush of pure relief. Tess threw the door open before Flynn had finished knocking, and she didn't even give him a chance to come inside before she threw herself at him.

He caught her, carried her into the apartment, and kicked the door shut behind him.

"I was so worried," she said, her voice too soft and quick. "I thought you'd be here hours ago, and then when you didn't show up I decided you weren't coming back at all."

"Did you really?" he asked in a voice that was tired and gruff and beautiful. "Did you really think you'd never see me again?"

She thought about the question for a minute, and then she remembered the expression she'd seen on his face as she'd walked off the bus this morning. "No."

Flynn put her on her feet and kissed her, deep and hard and tasting of recklessness. Her body responded quickly and acutely, as it always did when he touched her. She hadn't realized how much she needed to hold him, until he kissed her. How could she have missed him so soon?

The how didn't matter, not tonight. She kissed him

with everything she had, and she touched him. She held on to him as if she'd never let him go.

When he started to undress her, pulling her sweater over her head and unfastening her jeans, she backed toward the bedroom and reached for his belt buckle, tugging and unfastening and holding on. Her hands trembled, she was so shaken and frenzied. Flynn's hands shook, too, and she was quite certain that wasn't normal, for him.

Maybe he did love her, in the only way he knew how.

In a matter of minutes they were naked and lying on the bed, arms and legs entangled, mouths joined and frenzied. She arched toward him, bringing his body in alignment with hers, finding the place where they fit, so well. Flynn had come to her prepared, tonight. He'd tossed a handful of condoms onto the bedside table before falling into bed with her, and while he kissed her once again, he opened one foil pack with obvious impatience.

They had so much to say to one another, so many explanations needed to be made. But not now. Right now she just wanted him to make her feel good and desirable and loved. She wanted to forget everything that had happened today, with her body and Flynn's joined together.

She wrapped her legs around him, as he guided himself to her, and swayed up and into him to bring him deeper into her quivering body.

He loved her fast and hard, without any sweet words or promises about tomorrow. The gentleness she had seen from him in the past wasn't a part of this, not tonight when gentleness wasn't called for. This sexual encounter was raw, and basic, and they both needed it to be that way.

The bed shook, Tess gasped and clung and reached, and the man who loved her lifted her hips and drove deeper than before. She climaxed intensely, and Flynn came with her. She cried out, once, and he whispered her name in a grating voice. Only then did the world slow down, a bit. He ran his fingers through her hair, and kissed her cheek, and she held her palm against his hard, warm jaw. While they lay there, entwined and trying to find a way to breathe deep again, the charged air turned cooler. The bed was still again, as if it waited for what would come next.

Sex was so much easier than what came after, but tonight she wouldn't be a coward.

"I could love you, if you'd let me," she said as she caressed Flynn's jaw with trembling fingers.

"I can't afford to let you, Red. You're great, I like you more than I should, and when I'm inside you I can't imagine not seeing you tomorrow and the day after that and the day after that. But outside of this room we don't want the same things."

"I know," she whispered. She wanted a family; he wanted to be free of any obligations that might threaten his heart.

"Besides, I'm not all that lovable."

"That's debatable."

Flynn left her to go to the bathroom and dispose of the condom, and for a long, lonely moment she wondered if he was going to come back. He very well might not. He could've come to her for the release of sex alone, and now he might dress and leave, with a word of good-night or not. She wanted him to return to her, at least for a while. The bed was so big and empty and cold without him in it, and she dreaded the night when she'd once again be sleeping alone in it.

But tonight was not that night, thank goodness. He came back to her, crawled beneath the covers and pulled her body against his.

"When are you leaving?" she asked, trying her best to sound as if it didn't matter…and failing badly.

"Tomorrow afternoon, probably," Flynn answered. "There are going to be a lot of questions about what happened here today. I told Dr. Barber I'd stick around and assure the parents that Austin is no longer a concern."

She lifted her head to look down at him. "Is there any chance either of them will come back?" she asked.

Flynn shook his head. "They both survived the shooting, but they'll be in the hospital for a good long while, and then they're going away for a very long time." He drew her head down to his shoulder. "Still, a lot of parents are going to withdraw their kids from the school, and I can't say that I blame them. I don't understand why they were sent away from home in the first place. If my kid had survived…" He didn't say anything more, but then, he didn't have to.

Tess wrapped her arms around Flynn and held on tight. But she didn't clutch at him, as her instincts commanded. The last thing he wanted was a woman who would cling.

"What are you going to do about Laura?" he asked.

Tess closed her eyes. "I don't know. She thinks her mother is dead, that's what Jack told her. Jack's mother told me that her lawyer had arranged for a good family to adopt my daughter, that my baby would have a better life than either Jack or I could give her. I believed her. It was years before I knew that she and Jack had kept the baby, that they'd told her that her mother died when she was born."

"All the more reason she should know the truth."

She'd had this argument with herself a thousand times. "I signed away all my legal rights years ago, so I can't see how anything good can come of it. All I'll accomplish by telling is to add upheaval to Laura's life."

"What a load of crap," Flynn said in a low, dark voice. "She's your daughter, and she has a right to know."

"It's not that easy." She had gone over the possible scenarios in her mind so many times, she had them all memorized. None of them ended the way she wanted. She wanted to turn back time. She wanted her baby back. "She's thirteen years old, Flynn. I can't just waltz in and turn her reality upside down because I want to be a part of her life."

"It would be a shock at first, but her life would be better with you in it."

Her heart lurched. She wanted to believe that, she truly did. "I'm not so sure it would be."

Flynn rolled her onto her back and hovered above her. He studied her face, what he could see of it in the near dark. "I can't get my daughter back, Red. She's gone. If I had the chance, any chance at all, to change what happened to her, I'd do it, no matter what the cost. I wouldn't dye my hair brown so no one would recognize me, and hide in the background, and take what little tiny bit I could get from a distance."

"You've been snooping in my medicine cabinet."

"Don't change the subject."

She studied Flynn's face, so harsh and beautiful in the moonlight. She loved him, she wanted him in this bed and in her life for as long as he'd have her. But right now she wished he'd mind his own business. He made her face her fears head on. He asked the questions she didn't dare ask herself. Did the man never take the easy way out?

"What if Laura hates me?" she whispered. "What if she never forgives me for giving her up?"

"She'll get over it," he said with a confidence she didn't feel.

"But…"

"Her life will be better with you in it. I know that without doubt. Will it be a shock to find out that the mother she thought was dead isn't? Of course. Will she have questions for you that you won't want to answer? Without a doubt. But once you get past all that, she's going to love you."

"You can't be sure of that."

"I can, actually."

She wondered if he meant anything by that. Maybe that was his way of telling her that he loved her, a little. Then again, maybe she was putting her own spin on his words, because it was what she wanted so much.

Flynn drew the covers down and raked the palm of his hand up her torso, moving slowly and deliberately and stopping to caress one breast and then the other. His hands were large, the fingers long, the skin rough. She loved his hands.

"I'm not going to be able to sleep tonight," he said as his hand almost lazily caressed her.

"Neither am I." She closed her eyes as her body responded to his touch, as if she was familiar with the hands that aroused her, as if Flynn knew her body so well he knew just where to touch and tease.

"And I don't want to talk about tomorrow."

"Neither do I."

Flynn lowered his head and kissed her soft belly, and she quivered from head to toe. She felt as if he was already a part of her, and had been for years. Not just in body, but in heart. For a man who would likely claim he had no heart, Flynn was amazingly tender. Physically, and in the words he spoke, he revealed a powerful tenderness. His mouth moved against her skin, tasting and testing. His tongue flickered over her, in a gentle way that made her respond at her very core.

Flynn said he'd be gone, tomorrow. She didn't want to believe that a man who made her feel this way, who cherished and protected her child and others, who spoke in the dark about the daughter he'd lost and would do anything to get back, would really, truly leave her.

But she did.

Chapter 13

Sadie felt the rush of a sense of accomplishment, the kind that only came with the conclusion of a satisfactory job. She'd known all along that she couldn't leave the Benning Agency until Cal and Kelly were reunited—it would be her last job for the major, but likely not her last job. She wanted to be a good wife and mother, but man, she needed this rush. One way or another, eventually, she and Truman would work together. In the next election he'd be running for sheriff, and there would be all kinds of opportunities. But for now, she concentrated on the current rush.

They could've flown from Colorado to Georgia; they could've driven straight through and been at the school where the guys were working by yesterday. But Sadie's morning sickness and Truman's insistence that she rest and Kelly's determination that everything be just-so when she saw her brother again slowed them down.

Sadie watched as Kelly fiddled with her newly colored hair—back to the original color, a dark brown like Cal's—in the mirror. Instead of a waitress uniform or jeans and a T-shirt, she'd dressed in a conservative but very nice rust-colored dress, with three-quarter-length sleeves and a hem that hit below the knee, and pretty high heeled shoes. Like Cal was going to care what she was wearing!

The girl was indeed nervous, and with good reason. She hadn't seen Cal in a very long time. Kelly had been a child when he'd left home; he hadn't been much more than a child. A lot had happened in between—to him, and to her. If she wanted things just-so, then that's what she should have.

"All this time I've been running," Kelly said as she finished messing with her hair and turned to face Sadie, "I've been running from Quinn."

"Yeah, pretty much."

Kelly smiled, but there wasn't a lot of joy in it. "I wondered why the state of Texas wanted me so badly they'd chase me across the country for years. Every time I thought the feeling that I was being followed was my own imagination, someone would ask a nosy question or look at me funny, or I'd hear that someone had been asking about me, and I was off again."

Kelly was relieved that she hadn't been the cause of her stepfather's death, in spite of what he'd done to her, and she was grateful that her brother was alive. But her life had just changed dramatically, and that was going to take some adjustment.

"I can't wait to see Cal's face when we show up," Sadie said.

"Neither can I," Kelly responded softly, and with a touch of uncertainty.

Flynn was packed and ready to go. After he made the promised appearance at parents' day and did his best to assure them that their children were safe here, he'd be free to go.

Free to go. What a crock. He felt anything but *free*.

Austin's real name was Dale Emerson. Somehow that wasn't right. Made him sound like an accountant, or a office manager. For months he'd been drifting in and out of the area, staying for a few days to meet with his "daughter" and scouting out the campus until it felt like home. Thorndale was such a small town he couldn't stay long without drawing attention, but he had been a semiregular at the small motel at the edge of town.

Max had gotten Emerson to tell him the name of the business associate who'd hired him to take out Wyatt Martin, Bev's extremely rich father. Emerson's partner Melody, who refused to give up her real name, was keeping her mouth shut. It didn't matter what she called herself—she was going away for a long time. The world was a better place with her behind bars, but the price for putting her there had been a high one.

Dante looked like he'd been rode hard and put up

wet, sitting in the lounge of the men's dormitory with his gaze turned toward the window and the spring day beyond.

"Are you all right?" Flynn asked as he walked into the room and dropped his bag in the corner.

"No," Dante answered simply and honestly.

Flynn pulled up a chair and sat near the distraught man. "I know you liked Serena Loomis a lot, and I hate it that things turned out this way. If we'd seen it coming…"

"We didn't see it coming," Dante interrupted. "Austin veered from the usual M.O. and Serena paid the price. We thought he was a thief who'd killed when he was caught, but instead he was an assassin who stole to cover up his intentions. We screwed up, and Serena's the one who's dead." They were all taking the woman's death hard, but Dante was understandably the most affected.

"I didn't tell her why I was here, but I thought about it a couple of times. I figured once the job was over I could tell her, and she'd either kick my ass or be relieved that I wasn't a janitor. And then maybe I'd keep seeing her, if she'd have me. She wasn't my type, Major. Give me a brainless blonde and I'm a happy man. Loomis wasn't brainless or blond. She was a take charge woman with a real laugh and her own ideas, and I got her killed."

"It's not your fault, you know that."

"No, I don't know that." Dante turned his head and stared at Flynn with dark, emotionless eyes. "If either of them ever gets out, I'll be waiting. If Max Larkin makes a deal with those monsters in order to nab someone higher up, then I'll take care of them myself. They won't get away with what they did."

Flynn couldn't completely push down the terrifying thought that it could have been Tess in that gardener's shed. "If it comes to that and you need help, you know I'm with you."

Dante left his chair in a burst of energy he didn't know how to expend. "I'd give my right arm to get Serena back, and if I could trade places with her I would. It's not right, what happened to her. It's not right."

Flynn didn't know what to say, so he let Dante storm out of the room. The kid had never said "love," during his tirade, but the word hung in the air, bittersweet.

Once again, Flynn was gone when she woke up. At least this time he'd left a note. *See you later.* How romantic.

Not that she'd ever expected romantic from Flynn.

Tess brushed her teeth, then opened the medicine cabinet to look at the box of brown hair dye. Flynn could've taken it with him or tossed it out, but he hadn't. What she did today, or what she didn't do, was her decision.

Hiding would be easiest, she supposed. She could blend into the background, watch from a distance to see what things were really like with Laura and her father and her new stepmother, and then, maybe in a few weeks or months, she would decide what to do.

What if Jack panicked like some of the other parents and withdrew Laura from this school? There were other private schools he could send her to, and what were the odds that Tess could find work there, or nearby? And if she did, what would Laura think when she turned around and saw the cafeteria lady from the Frances Teague Academy at her new school?

Odds were that Jack wouldn't take Laura anywhere. After all, he hadn't felt it necessary to change his travel plans and come in last night, to see for himself that his daughter was truly safe.

For a few long minutes, Tess studied her reflection and the box of hair dye, alternately. She had changed in the past thirteen years, but not that much. She was older and some of the years showed on her face, but her features were the same. If Jack saw her, he'd almost certainly recognize her. And then what? Would he confess to Laura that he'd been lying to her all her life?

Tess showered, and dressed in her usual uniform. She tucked the hairnet in her pocket, and before she left the bathroom she chucked the box of hair color into the garbage can.

A good number of the parents were indeed soothed by Flynn's presence. He put on his best air of authority, and he smiled on occasion, and he assured them that the crisis had passed and all was well.

Dr. Barber was beside herself with worry, afraid that some of the more cautious parents would insist on withdrawing their daughters. A few did just that, and nothing Dr. Barber or anyone else said to them would change their minds. But most of the parents accepted that all was well, and that the Frances Teague Academy had employed the best available to keep their daughters safe.

In a way, Flynn was annoyed that Dr. Barber was so concerned about the financial bottom line. But he owned a business, too, and he knew too well that someone had to worry about the finances. Otherwise the Frances Teague Academy would cease to exist.

Flynn was surprised to see Bev Martin and her father in attendance. Since the man who'd hired Dale Emerson was now behind bars, like the two he'd hired, the danger was over. The business partner had hired Austin all on his own, for personal as well as professional reasons. Apparently there was money *and* a woman involved. A dangerous combination in any circumstance. Bev didn't want to miss her soccer match, and her father wouldn't deny her anything. Not today.

The man Flynn really wanted to see arrived late. Laura had been anxiously awaiting her father's arrival, and she ran to the parking lot to meet the car.

Did he despise Jack Stokes because the man hadn't bothered to make the trip yesterday? Or because of the things he'd done to Tess? Like it or not, both mother and daughter were important to Flynn, and he felt each slight to them as if it were his own. The two of them were everything he'd been so sure he didn't want. Commitment, responsibility. Love. Family.

Crap.

He hadn't seen Tess since leaving her sleeping early this morning, but then she and Mary Jo and two part-timers were in the kitchen, getting ready to serve lunch not only to the girls, but their parents, as well. He could go inside and say hello, but he hadn't done that. Not yet.

What was he going to say to her when he did see her again? The possibilities had been flitting and playing through his head all morning, and his conversation with Dante hadn't helped matters any.

It didn't matter how much a man didn't want to deal with those things he couldn't ever fix, now and then they broadsided him anyway. Like a ton of bricks, like a freight train coming out of nowhere…like a beautiful woman with a big heart and her bright—if occasionally irritating—daughter.

Laura dragged her father toward Flynn. The woman who trailed behind, bored and unsmiling, had to be the stepmother. She didn't look to be any older than twenty-five, and with her pale blond hair and model-pretty face and figure, she was the epitome of the rich man's trophy wife. And all Flynn could think of is what a poor substitute she was for Tess. As a woman, as a mother… in every way imaginable.

"This is Mr. Benning," Laura said breathlessly. "He's my substitute history teacher, because Mr. Hill got sick. At first I didn't like the way he taught class, but he's getting much better."

Flynn smiled. "Gee, thanks, kid."

"And I'm so glad he was here yesterday. He knew just what to do. Isn't it lucky that he was here?"

Jack Stokes offered his hand for a quick and seemingly obligatory shake, and Flynn took it. Laura didn't have to know that it hadn't been simple luck that had brought him to this school. Then again, she'd seen his weapon; she'd seen him in the midst of the investigation that had followed. Like her mother, Laura was smart. She had probably put the pieces of this puzzle together on her own. Some of them, anyway.

"Thank you, Mr. Benning," Stokes said.

"Just doing my job." The handshake was a quick one, and Flynn was glad to turn his attention to Laura. "You'll be glad to know that Mr. Hill will be back in the classroom on Monday morning."

Her smile faded. "Oh. I guess there won't be any more class outside, or pop quizzes, or lectures."

"Guess not," Flynn answered.

Laura wrinkled her nose, and then dismissed the unpleasantness. She turned to her father again, taking his sleeve in her grasp. "You have to meet Tess. Ms. Stafford, I mean. She was with me yesterday, and she was *so* nice and *so* cool headed. She was really, really great."

"Then I definitely want to meet her," Stokes said.

"Tess is pretty busy right now," Flynn said. "Why don't you introduce your Dad to her after lunch?" Tess didn't need to be blindsided by the man who had betrayed her and taken her child. When she was ready to face Jack, she would. Or else she wouldn't. Either way, she needed to know that Laura intended to introduce the woman who had been beside her during the crisis yesterday to her father.

"I'd like to speak with Dr. Barber," Stokes said, pointing to the headmistress who stood on the grassy area near the soccer field. "Mr. Benning, nice to meet you," he said halfheartedly. He looked down at Laura. "I'll catch up with you later, honey. I want you to introduce me to your English teacher. Your grades there aren't what they should be." He and his wife headed toward the busy headmistress, leaving Flynn and Laura alone in the parking lot.

He couldn't very well tell Laura that her father was an ass, but he sure considered it.

"Brittany, that's my stepmother, she wants to have kids soon," Laura said as she watched her father and his wife walk away, leaving her behind as they apparently always left her behind. "I know she wishes I wasn't around, and sometimes Dad tries to keep her happy by, you know, not spending too much time with me. When they have kids, I guess I'll really be the...the redheaded stepchild." She sounded so wistful, it broke Flynn's heart, a little. "Usually I look forward to summer vacation, but not this year."

"That sucks, kid," Flynn said in a lowered voice. His heart hitched. He could fix this one, dammit, if Tess would let him.

"My mother is dead," Laura added in a quick and heartbreakingly young voice. "Did I ever tell you that?"

"No, you didn't."

"She died when I was a baby, so I guess it was my fault. You know, something went wrong with the delivery and—"

"No," Flynn said sharply. He couldn't say much; it wasn't his place, or his decision. "I don't know what happened, but I'm sure whatever it was, it wasn't your fault."

Laura watched her father carry on a sedate discussion with Dr. Barber. "When I was little, I was so sure she wasn't really dead. I used to pretend that she just showed up at the door one day to take me. There could've been some kind of mix-up at the hospital," she said. "Or else she got amnesia and my dad only thought she was dead." And then she wrinkled her nose, in that way she had. "But my grandmother told me there aren't any such things as silly old fairy tales, and that I should accept reality and stop living with my head in the clouds."

Flynn's hands crawled into tight fists. "Did you ever see a picture of your mother?" he asked.

Laura shook her head. "No. I guess it was too painful for my dad to have them around. He must've loved her a lot, right?" She turned eyes, so much like Tess's, to him.

"You know, I've always been a big believer in fairy tales, myself," he said.

Before Laura could respond, her father called and waved to her. Apparently he was ready to talk to Stephanie McCabe about Laura's English grade. Flynn watched the girl run to her father. Halfway there, she turned and yelled at him. "Come to my soccer game this afternoon?"

"Wouldn't miss it!" he called back.

As he walked toward the main building Flynn wondered if Tess's hair was brown or red today. He wondered if she'd hide from Jack Stokes or meet him head-on. He wondered if she still believed in fairy tales.

Wondering about how she was going to handle the confrontation with the father of her child gave his brain an opportunity to wander away from his own dilemma.

How the hell was he going to walk away from these two redheads?

The truth hit him square in the gut. He couldn't walk away. Tess and Laura were his girls, in a way he had never expected was possible. They were *his*—and, by God, he was going to keep them.

Flynn stuck his head into the kitchen and looked directly at her. "Take a break?" he asked.

"We're very busy." Besides, she didn't know what to say to him.

"Five minutes."

Tess nodded to Mary Jo, and left the bustling kitchen to join Flynn in the hallway. "What is it?" she asked as she wiped chocolate from her hands onto the apron she wore. She got most of it, but not all.

She didn't like the expression on Flynn's face. The last thing she needed was another crisis, and it seemed that he was always surrounded by crisis. Either that, or he actually created it wherever he went.

He reached up and pulled off her hairnet, and he grinned as her undyed hair came tumbling down. "Way to go, Red."

"It doesn't mean I've made any decisions."

"I met Laura's father," he said, and the statement was accompanied with a grimace that told her very well what he thought of Jack.

"At least he showed up," Tess said.

Flynn leaned near her. "Doesn't Laura deserve better than *the least* any parent can give her?"

"Of course she does."

Flynn tucked the hairnet into her pocket. "I'm here to warn you. Laura wants to introduce you to her father. I convinced her to wait until after lunch."

"Thanks," she said, her voice soft.

"Not that you couldn't march out there right now and give him a piece of your mind. I wouldn't mind seeing that happen."

"Don't try to trick me into doing something I'm not ready to do," she said, her heartbeat increasing.

"I'm not here to trick you or coerce you."

"Then why are you here?"

"For this."

He kissed her on the mouth, in that way he had that made her knees and her will weaken, and then he laid his lips on the side of her neck. Having him here, having him touch her, made her feel stronger. Better. More in control, even though she had never shown any control where Flynn Benning was concerned.

"You smell like chocolate," he whispered against her throat.

She held on to Flynn, for a moment. A moment was all she had. The kitchen was waiting for her, and so was the biggest decision of her life. She had such a bad track record, where big decisions were concerned.

"Sorry. I have chocolate frosting all over my hands and my uniform."

"Don't apologize. I love the smell of chocolate."

Flynn kissed her mouth again, and she let herself get lost in it. He lifted her off her feet and kissed her, and by the time he put her down she was light-headed and wobbly kneed.

She didn't think he had the power to affect her any more strongly than he just had, and then he leaned down and rested his forehead against hers. "No matter what you decide to do about Laura, I'm still gonna love you."

And then he got down on one knee, and her heart almost came through her chest.

"What are you doing?" she asked hoarsely.

He grinned at her. "What does it look like I'm doing?"

Mary Jo stuck her head into the hallway, shouting, "Tess, your five minutes is—" And then she saw Flynn, down on one knee. "Never mind," she said with a wide grin. "We can carry on without you."

"Marry me," Flynn said in a confident and completely certain voice.

Tess began to shake her head. "No. No, I…"

"No," he repeated, and then he started to slowly rise.

"I'm wearing rubber-soled shoes and an ugly uniform and an apron smeared with chocolate, and when you found me I was wearing a hairnet, for goodness sake. I smell like chocolate, and…"

Flynn dropped back down to his knee. "So, that's not actually a *no,* is it?"

"I don't know," she whispered.

"If you're waiting for the perfect moment, then you

might as well say no," he said. "We might get a few of those in our lives, but not nearly enough. When they come along, you have to grab them and savor them and remember every little detail. You gave me some perfect moments, Tess, and I want to try for more. When I came here, I didn't think that was possible, not for me, but you make me want more."

A voice hissed from the kitchen doorway, *"Say yes."*

Tess turned toward Mary Jo, and the part-timers who had joined her, and shooed them away with one hand. Not that she thought they went far.

"I do love you," she said softly, when she and Flynn were relatively alone again.

He smiled. "That's a start. All you have to do now is say yes, Red."

She wanted to. *Yes,* bubbled up in her throat and teased her tongue, but when she opened her mouth to answer she said, "I can't."

Tess dropped down to her knees, to kneel before Flynn so they were almost eye-to-eye. She touched his cheek, which was already a little rough with pale brown stubble. He wasn't the kind of man to beg, or chase, or even to ask twice.

"It's true, I do want perfect, or as close as I can get."

"I'm not perfect, Red," he said.

"Neither am I. But I don't want you to ask me to marry you because you think I need fixing, or because you're still stirred up about what happened yesterday…or just because you're relieved that I'm not dead."

"That's not…"

"I saw Mangino before he left, Flynn. He's hurting. You're his friend, so I know you saw it, too."

"Of course I did."

"I remember how you said that could have been me."

"That's not why I asked you to marry me."

"Maybe not," she whispered. "But I can't be certain of that right now. And there's the matter of babies, Flynn. I want them. One, two, three…I don't know. But I won't live my life afraid of what might happen. I've lived that way long enough."

She leaned forward and kissed him. "I love you," she said when she drew away and dropped her hands from his face. "I thank you for that, because I never thought I'd love anyone this way again. When all this is over and behind us, if you still want to ask…the answer will be different."

The problem was, she was pretty sure Flynn wasn't the waiting around type.

Chapter 14

Every fairy tale needed a Prince Charming. Flynn had never considered himself a particularly charming guy, but where his girls were concerned he was willing to give it a try.

One princess at a time.

If he were younger, more sensitive or less self-assured, he'd be hightailing it out of town at this very moment. But when Tess had told him all the reasons she couldn't marry him, he'd been watching her eyes. She loved him; she wanted him. Everything else would come together, sooner or later.

She hadn't been in the dining hall at lunchtime, so there had been no opportunity for Laura to introduce her father to the woman who had been with her during the traumatic events of yesterday. Tess was in her room, he knew, trying to decide what to do. Maybe she was even flirting with that box of hair dye.

He started a couple of times to check up on her, but only made it halfway up the stairs before retreating. It wasn't any of his business how she handled this situation.

But when she still didn't show after an hour or so, he ran to the second floor, knocked soundly and opened that door before she had a chance to open it or tell him to go away.

Tess was still dressed in her white uniform. She stood in her little kitchenette, pouring herself a cup of coffee, as if a caffeine overdose was going to make the situation any better. She'd kicked off her shoes, her hair was down and even from here he could spot a speck of chocolate icing on her throat.

"If you came here to try to talk me into facing Jack…" she began hotly.

"Nope," he said as he walked toward her. "I didn't come to ask you to marry me again, either. This is not a stress-inducing social call, I hope."

She relaxed visibly, muttering a soft, "Oh."

Flynn took the coffee cup out of her hand and set it aside. He kissed her, and she let him. Man, he loved the way she let him kiss her, as if she trusted and wanted him with a completeness he had never known. After a few minutes, he unbuttoned her uniform to the waist, and she didn't tell him to stop. His hand slipped inside to grasp her, skin to skin. To touch her. He unfastened her bra and caressed her breasts while they kissed, and she moaned low in her throat. A hundred decisions were yet to be made, but this wasn't one of them.

She spiraled out of control, and so did he. It was so easy with Tess. So right.

After licking a spot of chocolate from her throat, he whispered, "No matter what happens, everything is going to be all right."

"How can you…"

"I don't know how, or when, but it's going to be all right."

"You can't possibly *know*…"

"I love you, Tess. Right now that's enough. It has to be, doesn't it? It's all we've got that matters."

"I love you, too," she whispered.

He lifted her skirt and pushed her panties down and off, and she unbuckled and unzipped his pants. Everything else might be screwy, but this they could do. Tess tried to tug him toward the bedroom, but Flynn stood his ground and lifted her off her feet. He braced her against the wall, lifted her legs to position them around his hips, and guided himself into her.

He hadn't been inside a woman without a condom in too many years to count, but it was right, for this woman and this time. Tess was surprised, at first, but she tightened her hold on him and gently moved her hips against his. They moved that way, slow and easy, for a few minutes. Her body wrapped around his felt so good, in so many ways, that he didn't want it to end.

She moved faster, and so did he, and then they came together, fast and hard. He climaxed inside her, and felt the gentle pulse of her body around his, as she milked and squeezed him.

Everything slowed, and he rested his forehead against hers. "Loving you makes me unafraid."

Most of his life was in an uproar, but the soccer game put a smile on his face. The Frances Teague Academy Ladybugs did not have the tradition of a winning team, not in the middle school division or the high school. Apparently their last coach had taught them that their best effort and sportsmanship made them all winners. Cal had a different coaching style.

Flynn tried not to laugh. Cal was really getting into his job as soccer coach, pacing the sidelines and yelling at the girls, and patting them on the back when they came to the bench. You'd think it was a battlefield, not a soccer field.

Cal had seen enough battlefields in his life; he deserved a little soccer field time.

Some of the methods the Ladybugs used were less than entirely ethical. Flynn saw the occasional elbow thrown, though it was always a discreet move made when the officials were facing the other way. Laura very delicately stuck out her foot, one time, and tripped an opposing player. And then she took the ball and ran with it.

The game was almost over, and the Ladybugs were actually ahead by two goals. Even Dr. Barber was excited. During the first half of the game she had looked a tad concerned by the girls' unusual new methods. But winning put a whole new spin on things.

When he heard the shuffle of a footstep in the grass, he knew it was Tess. Sure enough, she stepped up beside him. She'd showered and changed clothes, after he'd left her. He couldn't help but picture the way he'd left her—half-dressed, face flushed, hair wild, lips swollen. Her hair was down but neatly combed. She'd used a little bit of makeup, and she wore navy blue pants and a white sweater. All in all, she looked quite respectable.

"Hi, Red. Change your mind about making an honest man out of me?"

She looked up at him with clear, green eyes that seemed a tad fearless today; that had to be a good sign. "No. I have to get a few things in my life straight before I can even think about us."

"Laura," he said.

She nodded. "Laura."

Tess stood with him and watched the game. Jack and his trophy wife were standing almost halfway down the field, only halfheartedly paying attention. Tess didn't make a move in that direction. She watched the field, and flinched a little when Laura used a little elbow on a player from the other team.

"Is that legal?" she asked.

"Not really."

Laura took the ball and ran with it, and this time she scored a goal. It was her first of the game, probably her first ever, and she celebrated as she made her way back to the center of the field.

The game would be over in a matter of minutes. Seconds, maybe. Tess looked up at him again. "I don't have any right to ask you to come with me when I face Jack, but…"

"I'm there. You don't even have to ask."

She nodded, edged a little bit closer, and then she took his hand and threaded her fingers through his. For strength, maybe, or for comfort. Maybe just because. Just because suited him fine.

When the final whistle sounded, the Ladybugs celebrated. Cal was in the middle of it all, smiling and proud and gratified.

It was Flynn's job to notice things, so when the car pulled into the parking lot his eyes shifted. Familiar car; familiar driver. What were Sadie and Truman doing here? With his luck, she was here to quit. Losing Cal and Sadie in the span of one week was going to be tough.

But he couldn't be angry. It was what they wanted. They were both happy in a way he had never thought they'd be.

Sadie and Truman exited their car…and one of the rear doors opened.

She didn't look a whole lot like the old high school picture Cal carried with him, but Kelly bore a striking resemblance to her brother. The three of them stood by the car and searched the campus, and it didn't take them long to find Cal, at the middle of the soccer team's celebration.

Unaware of what was going on in the parking lot, what was about to happen to Cal, Tess took a deep breath and tugged on Flynn's hand. Together they headed down the sideline toward Jack Stokes. Halfway there, she released his hand, but he didn't fall behind.

Cal was going to be fine—better than fine—and Tess needed him. He was right behind her, and always would be—if she'd let him.

Stokes looked down the sidelines, and at first he didn't recognize the mother of his daughter. That blissful ignorance didn't last, though. He did a double take, and his eyes went wide, and he looked like a good stiff breeze would knock him over. As Tess and Flynn drew close, he said to his wife, "Honey, I have some aspirin in the glove compartment. Would you fetch me a couple? I have a splitting headache." He handed Brittany the keys to his car, and with a very soft huff she left.

"Hi, Jack," Tess said softly.

"Teresa." He looked at her, and then up at Flynn. "I didn't expect to see you here."

"I guess not."

The silence that followed was uncomfortable, strained and heavy. Flynn stood back and waited. If Tess needed him, he'd know. For now, she was doing just fine.

Stokes had the good grace to look guilty. He actually took a small step toward Tess. "I'm sorry. I would have done things differently if I'd had the guts to stand up to my mother. Back then, I didn't."

"How is she?" Tess asked in a tight voice.

"Not well," Stokes said softly. He glanced toward the field, where the team continued to celebrate.

Flynn glanced in that direction, too. Sadie, Truman and Kelly were making their way toward the field and Cal, but he hadn't seen them yet.

"I guess you want to tell her?" Stokes asked sharply.

"Yes."

"It won't be easy. She thinks you're dead."

"Thanks for that, by the way," Tess responded, her anger rising to the surface. "It doesn't make this any easier."

"It wasn't my idea," Jack said defensively. "And by the time I had the guts to buck my mother, it was too late."

Too late were not the words Tess wanted to hear.

Laura ran to her father, with a smile for Tess and Flynn along the way. "Did you see? I scored a goal!"

"That was great, honey," Stokes said with a wan smile.

"Yeah, if not for the elbow and the trip, I'd make you player of the game," Flynn said with a smile.

Laura responded with a grin of her own, and at that moment she didn't look awkward and gawky and uncertain. She looked like her mother.

Stokes put an arm around his daughter's shoulders and led her away from the soccer field. Tess and Flynn followed closely. Laura was confused, glancing around almost nervously, as her father made his way toward the track where Tess liked to take her exercise.

Flynn glanced back, just as Cal turned and saw Kelly step onto the soccer field. He didn't move, for a moment, and she stopped there on the sidelines. It was a good thing, seeing Kelly and Cal find each other again. For them, it was one of those rare perfect moments.

Cal didn't need him, not now, but Tess did. Flynn turned his back on the reunion and followed Tess and Laura and the man who had ripped them apart thirteen years ago.

They found a quiet spot that was pretty and green and secluded, and Jack Stokes turned to his daughter. The expression on his face was hard, and more than a little scared. "You're a big girl now, Laura, and…and there are certain things you deserve to know." His face went pale. "None of us is without fault, and in the past we've all made mistakes. We've all…made decisions we regret." He looked over Laura's shoulder to Tess. "You want to help out here? I don't have any idea how to do this."

Laura turned to face Tess. Did she sense the truth, in the same way she had known as a child that her mother wasn't dead? It seemed that Laura held her breath, dreading and hoping and wondering. Tess was just as frozen, even though she had played this moment over in her mind again and again.

Flynn stepped past Tess and draped his arm around Laura's shoulder. The two redheads were face-to-face, and a nervous Stokes watched. They didn't know how to start, but Flynn did. He looked into Laura's green eyes, smiled and said, "Once upon a time…"

In the movies, Cal and Kelly probably would've run into each others arms to rising, emotional music. Sadie waited for that to happen—without the music, of course—but it didn't. Instead the brother and sister stepped toward one another almost cautiously. The girls from the soccer team had all gone their own way, and Cal had been left alone in the middle of the field.

Kelly stepped with caution, since her high-heeled shoes were not made for walking in the grass. Cal walked slowly because he didn't yet understand what he thought he saw.

"Kelly?" he said, as if he wasn't quite sure he could believe what his eyes told him.

The girl nodded as she stepped closer to her brother. "Yeah."

They stopped for a moment, and then Cal laughed and swept his little sister off her feet and spun her around. "Thank God. I swear, girl, I thought we were never going to find you."

Kelly was breathless when Cal finally put her back on her feet.

They had a lot of catching up to do, and Sadie's job was done. She took Truman's hand and backed away, but Cal caught her eye.

"Hold it right there," he commanded, and he left Kelly behind to walk toward Sadie with that fierce expression she knew so well on his face. "You didn't call? You didn't think to warn me?"

"I wanted to surprise you," Sadie said with a sly smile.

Cal lifted her off her feet, too, though with a tad less enthusiasm than he had shown for his sister. "I hate surprises," he said softly.

"Yeah, I know."

"I will never be able to thank you enough," he said as he released her.

"Go get reacquainted with your sister." She patted him on the cheek before turning away to take Truman's hand. Together, she and her husband walked back toward the parking lot.

"You can quit now, right?" Truman said as they left Cal and Kelly hugging once again.

"I suppose," Sadie said. "For a while."

"For a while."

Sadie grinned, and glanced back over her shoulder once. It was a good feeling, to accomplish something that changed two nice people's lives for the better. "Well, when you're elected sheriff, you'll need a lead investigator...right?"

Laura had been surprised to learn the details of her birth, and she'd cried, a little. She'd been understandably shocked, but she'd accepted the truth quickly and completely. There hadn't been a quick and easy ending, like a fairy tale, but they were working on it. They didn't have all the bugs worked out, and maybe they never would.

But they were trying.

Lunch was over, and preparations for dinner hadn't yet begun. Since it was Saturday, the evening meal would be simple. Soup and sandwiches, tonight, along with brownies she'd made this morning. Tess wiped down one particularly messy table, her mind straying to the subject that had been plaguing her, lately.

In the week after he'd left the Frances Teague Academy, Flynn had called her twice. Their conversations had been brief and friendly. He'd asked about Laura, and Bev, and some of his other students, and then he'd ended the conversations abruptly.

The following week, he'd called just once. Again he'd asked about Laura and Bev, and she'd asked him how Mangino was doing. Better, Flynn said, but not yet himself. He brought her up to date on Murphy and Cal, and she told him how the girls were all comparing Mr. Hill's teaching methods to his. They missed him. She did, too, but she didn't say so.

In that third phone call, she told him that she wasn't pregnant, just in case he was worried…not that he'd sounded worried. Or had bothered to ask.

In those three phone calls, Flynn hadn't once mentioned marriage or said he loved her or talked about coming back. She'd been right when she'd suspected that the only reason he'd asked her to marry him that day was because he was still reeling from what had happened to Serena Loomis.

He wanted to protect her, he wanted to fix her life. That was very sweet, but it wasn't love. But oh, she missed him. She missed him more than she'd imagined she could.

"There you are!" Laura said brightly as she and Bev burst into the dining hall.

Tess lifted her head and smiled at her daughter.

"Here," Bev said, thrusting a long, flowing plastic bag falling from a coat hanger toward Tess. "You have to put this on. Quick!"

"I don't want to take that, my hands are dirty," she said. "What have you girls got there?"

Bev lifted the end of the plastic bag to reveal the skirt of a long, champagne-colored dress.

"Where did you get that? Laura, did your father . . ."

"No," Laura took her hand and dragged her toward

the doorway. "Come on, Mom. He's waiting. You don't want to make him wait too long, do you?" In a month they had gone from Ms. Stafford to Tess to the occasional Mom or Mother, depending on Laura's mood. There were more Moms lately, which was nice.

"Who's waiting?" Her heart skipped a beat, and she knew. Before Laura said a word, she *knew.*

"Mr. Benning, of course. He said this time everything would be perfect. You should see him. He looks like James Bond!"

Tess held back her response that Flynn *was* James Bond, in his own way.

As they rushed up the steps to her apartment, Bev said, "Mr. Benning really does look very nice. And he has—"

"Don't tell everything," Laura interrupted. "You'll spoil the surprise."

The girls escorted Tess to her apartment, where in high-pitched excited voices they instructed her to change her clothes. When the dress was out of the bag, Tess shook her head several times. It was too fancy, too low-cut, too expensive.

But it was also exquisite, and the right size, and it didn't take a lot of encouragement from the girls to persuade her to put it on.

A gown like this one couldn't be just thrown on. It required a shower, the proper shoes and a touch of makeup. A fancy hairstyle would be nice, but she didn't think Flynn would wait that long. An hour after the girls had run into the dining hall, she was ready.

As ready as she'd ever be.

"Mom, you look beautiful!" Laura exclaimed as they left the apartment together.

"Yeah," Bev said softly. "Really beautiful."

For the first time in a long while she felt beautiful, and it had nothing to do with a fancy dress or a little bit of makeup. Flynn was here for her, and he'd come in style. She should've expected no less.

Tess held her breath as she stepped outside, into the warm spring day that smelled of new growth and flowers. The sky was a bright, clear blue, the lawn and the trees were spring green…and Flynn stood in the middle of it all, on a section of the winding sidewalk just a few feet away. Dressed in a tuxedo and carrying a huge bouquet of red roses, he did look a little like James Bond. Or a very nicely dressed swashbuckler.

His face was solemn at first, and she suspected she'd left him waiting too long. He was *not* a patient man. But as she drew closer he smiled at her. "How's this for perfect, Red?"

And with those words it was as if he'd never been gone. "As usual, you've gone above and beyond."

"I'm a man who's willing to do whatever it takes to get what I want. Get used to it."

She couldn't wipe the smile from her face. What he wanted was *her.*

"You're gorgeous," he said.

"So are you."

He handed her the roses and got down on one knee, again, and then he offered her one palm. She laid her hand on that palm, and he closed his long fingers over hers.

"You make me want a better life, and if you'll say yes, that life starts here and now. Marry me."

They didn't have anything settled between them. He had a dangerous job; she wanted babies and he didn't; she didn't want to leave the daughter she'd just found and claimed.

But no matter what the obstacles were, she did want Flynn. For better or for worse. He had been right all along. Somehow, it would work. "Yes," she said softly.

He took an outrageously large diamond solitaire from his pocket and slipped it on her finger, and then he stood and kissed her. Since others were watching…a *lot* of others, though they maintained a proper distance…the kiss didn't last nearly long enough.

"I realized while you were gone that I had perfect with you from that first kiss," she said. "This is all very nice, but you didn't have to go to so much trouble. If you'd asked me to marry you while I was in the middle of serving lunch, and you were covered in scalloped potatoes and I was covered in chocolate…I still would've said yes."

"Nice to know," he answered. "Still, the effort wasn't wasted."

"Of course not. This is beautiful and special and I'll never forget it."

He put his arm around her and they began to walk back toward the main building. "Yeah, and it'll give us a story to tell our children, when they're old enough. We won't tell them exactly what happened afterward, but…"

Tess stopped walking and turned to him. "Did you say *our children?*"

He grinned at her and swept her off her feet. Literally, this time. "Yep. I haven't been sitting around twiddling my thumbs for the past month, you know. I've been busy."

"Busy," she repeated skeptically.

"Cal was going to quit, but I convinced him to stay on and run the agency from headquarters."

"I thought that was your job."

"It was. Now it's Cal's job. His first step was to hire his sister, but I would've hired her myself so that's not a problem as far as I'm concerned. Besides I don't have time to worry about day-to-day operations of the business. I'm going back to school in the fall. There's a college just about an hour from here, and I only need a year or so of classes."

"To do what?"

"To get my teaching degree. I have a degree, I have all the qualifications to be a substitute, but if I want to teach full-time I need a few more classes."

He carried her toward the main building, like a bride being carried to her new home. "So you want babies, and you're going back to school, and you've given up your job."

"Yep. Money's not a problem," he said quickly, as if he suspected that was why she sounded uncertain. "I have a lot of it, actually. The agency has been very successful, and I haven't had anything to spend money on for a while. If I'm going to be a family man, I can't very well go running off to chase bad guys all the time."

Flynn carried her inside, and thank heavens—no one

followed them in. The girls all headed back to their own dormitories. For them, the show was over. For her, it had just begun.

"Are you sure? About the babies, I mean?" Tess asked as Flynn carried her up the stairs. Just a few weeks ago, he had insisted that he didn't want to take that chance again.

"If I wasn't sure, I wouldn't be here," he answered. "I wouldn't ask you to marry me unless I was ready to give you everything you want and deserve. It's what I want, too," he added in a lowered voice. "I didn't realize that's what I wanted until I tried to picture what my life would be like from here on out without you in it. I want it all, Red."

"So do I." She'd never imagined that she could truly have everything she wanted. Laura, Flynn, babies. She leaned in close and whispered in his ear. "You make me unafraid, Flynn. I love you so much."

Outside the door to her apartment, he said, "I think we should get started on that first baby right about now. What do you say?"

She buried her face against his neck, smiled, kissed and answered.

"Damn skippy."

* * * * *

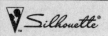

COMING NEXT MONTH

#1375 RAMIREZ'S WOMAN—Beverly Barton
The Protectors
Mocorito's presidential candidate Miguel Ramirez wanted a female bodyguard to pose as his fiancée—and Dundee agent J. J. Blair was most definitely female. Though neither one of them welcomed their instant attraction, they both seemed helpless to resist it. With political threats placing their lives on the line, would they be strong enough to risk their hearts, too?

#1376 DEFENDING THE RANCHER'S DAUGHTER—Carla Cassidy
Wild West Bodyguards
While growing up, Katie Sampson despised the young, handsome Zack West for stealing her father's attention. Now she needed Zack's help to solve the mystery behind her father's death—and the plots against her life. Zack agreed to defend the rancher's daughter, but before long he feared that once the case ended, so would their passion....

#1377 THE BEAST WITHIN—Suzanne McMinn
PAX
The thing Keiran Holt feared most lived inside him—and possibly could cause him to harm the woman he'd married But Paige wasn't the only one who had spent two years searching for her missing husband. Would the agency they had once loved capture him before they saved their once-passionate marriage... and tamed the beast within?

#1378 IN THE DARK WATERS—Mary Burton
Kelsey Warren had fled her hometown eight years ago to get away from her family's shame and Sheriff Mitch Garrett—a man who claimed he didn't love her. Now Kelsey was back, and eager to solve the mystery surrounding her mother's disappearance. Amidst uncovering clues, the two hit it off once again. This time around, was Mitch in it for the long haul?

SIMCNM0605